When you're at rock bottom, when life can't get any worse ... you don't see the point of carrying on ...

... until someone walks into your world and makes all the difference.

A Brightness out of the Blue
by Jill Atkins

Published by Raven Books
An imprint of Ransom Publishing Ltd.
Unit 7, Brocklands Farm, West Meon, Hampshire GU32 1JN, UK
www.ransom.co.uk

ISBN   978 178591 305 1
First published in 2016

A
Brightness
out of the
Blue

Jill Atkins

1

Rain soaks through my thin coat and trickles down my neck as I hurry along the darkening streets of Madebury. Head down, arms wrapped around my body to try and stop the shivering, I'm totally tensed up against the cold, focused on getting there as quickly as possible.

Suddenly, I halt. My hand instinctively clasps over my mouth. A dead blackbird lies in front of me, its head at a strange angle, its yellow beak brilliant against the dull pavement. I stare at it for a moment, wondering how the poor thing broke its neck. I swallow hard, trying to blot it from my mind, then I carefully step over it and walk on.

There is a roar behind me. A car coming too fast races by, splashing dirty gutter water over my legs. Cursing the driver, I quicken my pace as the lights of the café come into view on the opposite side of the street, like a beacon shining out against the murkiness of the November afternoon.

I reach the door and burst in. Blinking in the sudden brightness inside the café, I stamp my feet and strip off my coat. Then, leaving a trail of drips across the floor, I order a cappuccino from Luigi at the bar, make for the empty table by the window and sit down.

Argh! I recoil at my reflection in the glass – strands of long black hair clinging to both sides of my stone-grey face. My mouth is set in a thin, hard line. Dark eyes are frowning angrily back at me.

I bite my lip to stop the tears that well up. This is not the life I've dreamed of. I turn from the window and shut my eyes.

I'm six years old, with Mum at the bird sanctuary. A wire cage as big as a building. We step inside. Birdsong. Flowers. Tall trees. Through the branches, brilliant sunlight creates intricate yellow patterns on a deep purple path. We tiptoe, hand-in-hand, beneath the trees, dodging the patterns as the leaves flicker in the breeze. An eagle owl soars high. Suddenly, it swoops down, straight at us. I scream and cling to Mum. Then we laugh as the owl swings away.

'Nothing to be afraid of.' Mum holds me tight. 'You're safe with me.'

The rattling of a cup and saucer brings me back to the present. I open my eyes and dry my tears. How I'd love to go back in time, to feel Mum's arms around me, to escape from this living hell.

I begin to shiver. My jeans cling icily to my legs and my feet feel numb inside my waterlogged trainers. I'm relieved Luigi doesn't speak as he ambles over, plonks down the coffee and takes my money. I wrap my hands around the cup and feel its warmth seeping into me. I glance around. The café is quite full, yet strangely quiet. Or is it just my black mood?

I glance at my watch. I have almost two hours before I need to leave. I'd have liked something to eat, but coffee is all I can afford. It's my only luxury, once a week, my comfort zone, a shot of energy on my way to work. Sighing, I concentrate on the froth in my cup, stirring it and watching the swirl of the liquid, wishing it would whisk me away.

Is it a powerful wishing potion, one that will grant me anything I want?

I turn back to the window. Blanking out the reflected image of myself, I stare through the glass at the depressing scene. It has stopped raining at last. Satin-smooth puddles mirror the traffic lights on the corner – red, amber, green. A man closes his umbrella as he hurries by.

Suddenly, something catches my eye. The faintest flicker of light. I crane my neck to see what it is. A little white-haired, wizened woman is shuffling slowly and unsteadily past, smartly dressed in expensive-looking clothes and black boots. I take in every detail, even noting her matching leather handbag.

And then I see the ring. I lean towards the glass. A diamond ring on her finger, flickering, flashing in a car's headlights. And the diamonds look enormous. It must be worth a fortune!

Why should that old woman have a ring like that while I have nothing? Anyway, she's taking a risk. Anyone could attack such a vulnerable woman and steal the ring. Anyone …

There is something intriguing about the old lady and I can't help watching her closely, curious.

Suddenly, as she totters past the café door, she trips. I smother a nervous giggle as she lurches forward, waving her arms in the air in an attempt to save herself. Like a slow motion replay. Then, there she is, on the pavement in a crumpled heap.

Before I realise what I'm doing, I'm on my feet, pulling on my coat and hurrying to the door.

'Are you all right?' I ask as I step outside.

The old woman sits up, clutching her handbag. Her dazed eyes stare up at me. In the light from the doorway, I see splashes of mud on her face. There is blood on both her knees.

'Yes, dear,' she whispers. 'I'll be fine.'

But she doesn't look all right. I quickly flick my hair behind my ears and move forward. There is a faint scent of lavender as I reach down and place my hands under the old woman's armpits. Light as a bird, all skin and bone, the poor old thing winces and cries out as I pull her to her feet.

'Have you got far to go?' I ask.

'No … left at the corner … ' She points. 'Not far from there.'

'Hold my arm,' I say. 'I'll see you home.'

A moment later, we begin to move unsteadily along the street. The woman trembles and grips my arm tightly. Her nails dig like talons into my wrist. I feel a bony elbow jabbing my ribs. A moment ago, she had felt so easy to lift. Now she weighs me down as we struggle slowly along. At each step, I hear a slight rasping of her breath.

Yet, despite the woman's frailty, there is something about her I can't explain. At her touch, a ripple of excitement has shot through my body like an electric current, making me tingle all over.

As soon as we turn the corner, I realise I've never been in this street before. There are no shops – just wide gateways, long front gardens and large houses. Trees stand stark and leafless along the side of the road. Brown and gold leaves cover the pavement in a broad waterlogged carpet. I tread carefully, aware that we could slip easily. Street lamps cast their pools of orange glow at intervals along the road and, as we pass beneath the first one, our bodies cast a grotesque two-headed shadow that stretches out over the leaves in front of us. As we stumble along, it grows longer and slowly fades to nothing.

At last, the old woman stops at a black wrought-iron gate.

'Here we are.' She lets go of my arm and leans heavily on the gate, as if she is trying to regain her strength.

I peer through the gloom. Behind a wilderness of tangled bushes, dark rectangular windows stare blindly out at me from the high red-brick walls of a house. Tall stone pillars guard the front entrance and in one corner a round, pointed turret stretches upwards like Rapunzel's tower, its single window as sightless as the rest. A creeper entwines itself around the whole building as if trying to choke it.

'You live *here*?' I whisper.

Suddenly, I notice two luminous eyes glowing out from the doorstep. A shadowy shape slowly slinks towards us. Then, as it reaches the light of the street lamps, a black cat materialises, like The Cheshire Cat. Except this cat has no smile as it rubs the side of its face on the gate post.

The old lady turns to me.

'Thank you so much, dear,' she says. 'I'll be all right now. What's your name, so I can remember you?'

'Ella.'

'I'm Martha.'

I presume I am being dismissed, but I feel drawn to this old woman, as if she has me on some kind of invisible cord. A shiver passes right through me and I feel slightly dizzy, overwhelmed by a peculiar and inexplicable sensation that Martha might somehow change my life.

2

I know I should leave, but my feet refuse to budge. I smile at Martha, desperately hoping that my instincts are right; that there *is* something special about her; that the chance won't slip away.

'Goodbye, then,' I whisper, wishing very hard that something will happen so I can stay.

All at once, Martha crumples. For the second time, the old woman is on the ground, her bag clutched tightly to her chest. She lies totally still, eyes closed. Is she dead? I stare, stunned. Has my wish done that?

Then Martha moans and her eyelids flutter. I shake myself to get rid of the beginnings of panic as I lift her again. I push the gate open with my foot and half-carry, half-drag her into the front garden, the cat leading the way. Martha clings to my arm more fiercely and painfully than before, and several times we stagger and almost fall on the uneven path.

'How do you cope,' I ask, 'when you don't have me to hang on to?'

Martha doesn't reply. She seems to be concentrating on reaching the house. She is struggling with her breathing as we reach rough steps and begin to climb. Inside the porch, the darkness is so thick I can almost touch it. I feel a prickly sensation all over my skin as I grope my way to the door. In spite of her weakness, there is a feeling of magic about her.

'My key,' Martha whispers. 'In my pocket.'

She trusts me completely, I think, as I push my hand deep into Martha's coat pocket and pull out a long, cold metal key. Its teeth feel rough against my fingers and I can't help closing my eyes for a second, hoping it is going to open up a better life for me.

'Will you unlock for me, dear?'

I bend down and feel for the keyhole, inserting the key and turning it. The loud click echoes back to me from inside the house and the door creaks as I tentatively push it open.

Total darkness. I inhale deeply. A damp, musty smell.

Autumn. A walk in the woods with Mum and Dad. A lifetime ago. I carry a basket, half-full of mushrooms. Mum knows what is safe to collect. She has shown me several poisonous toadstools, deadly enough for a witch's brew.

I hear rustling. Rats? I shudder and quickly run my fingers along the inside wall, feeling for the switch. Expecting brilliance, I shade my eyes in anticipation, but the single light bulb is just enough to reveal the vast, high-ceilinged hall.

'In you go.' Martha releases my arm.

Stepping inside, I immediately have the sensation that someone is watching me. I look around at the faded wallpaper, the low armchair, the old-fashioned hat-stand and the oval mirror on the wall.

Then I see it. A huge, sleek black bird sits silent and still on the newel post at the bottom of the wide staircase, its slate-grey eyes gleaming. I gasp, then, recovering, stare back without flinching.

'Don't worry about Corvus.' Martha's voice resounds across the hall.

I turn to her. 'Corvus?'

'The raven. He's been with me these sixty years and never done anyone any harm.'

I look more closely, blink then frown. Sixty years? Do ravens live that long? Then I smile. I've been trying to out-stare a stuffed bird.

Martha comes inside and shuts the door. She seems steadier now and more confident, as she takes off her coat and hangs it on the hat-stand. I guess she is glad to be home.

'You're so wet and bedraggled, dear. You must have been caught in that deluge. Come into the kitchen and dry yourself in front of the fire.'

'But … ' I protest, but not very loudly. I like the thought of being warm and dry.

'Why don't you stop for a cup of tea?'

My resistance is low. My need to stay is taking over, even though I know I only have a little time now before leaving for work.

'OK. Thanks.'

Taking my arm again, Martha flicks on more dim lights and we follow a narrow corridor to the kitchen. It's like walking into a museum, with its cream walls, square butler sink, wooden draining board and a large black kitchen range that takes up most of the far wall. Martha pulls out a chair from under the oak table in the middle of the room, deposits her handbag on the table and sits down heavily. She leans back and sighs.

'Take your coat off,' she says. 'Put it by the range to dry.'

Peeling off my coat, I hang it on a hook at the side of the range and rub my hands together in the warmth from the fire. Then I remember the blood on Martha's legs.

'I'll bathe your knees,' I say. 'They must be sore. Then I'll make some tea.'

I fill a kettle from a single tap at the sink. There is a pile of dirty dishes on the draining board, quite a lot for one old woman, I would have thought. I put the kettle on the range then, fetching a bowl of water and a cloth, I kneel in front of Martha.

'I'll try not to hurt,' I say, as I begin to wash out the mud and grit.

'Thank you, dear.' Martha places her hands in her lap.

And there is the ring again. Dazzling, stunning. I can't take my eyes off it.

'You like my ring?'

I look up, startled, guilty, but Martha's blue eyes are sparkling like the ring.

'It's beautiful,' I whisper as I dry Martha's knees. 'It must be very valuable.'

'Yes, it is.'

'Why do you wear it out in the street? It could have been stolen.'

'I've been to visit my elderly sister today and she loves to see it,' says Martha. 'It reminds her of our mother. The ring was hers.'

I swallow hard and bite my lip, trying not to show the emotion that is welling up inside. But she has noticed.

'What is it, dear?'

I'm surprised at how quick-witted Martha is. I shake my head, too full to speak.

'Did I say something to upset you?'

I shut my eyes and bow my head.

'Nothing to be afraid of. You're safe with me.'

'Do you want to talk about it?' Martha's hand gently strokes my hair. Such a wonderful comforting sensation. I've missed it so much.

I feel confused. I hardly know Martha, but I feel

bewitched. I badly want to pour everything out to her; about Dad's hateful new wife; about my job; about my new lodgings with Velcro, Bea and Tilly; about Mum. Yes, especially about Mum.

It might take away the pain.

The piercing whistle of the kettle breaks the spell. I jump up and rush to the cooker to turn it off, the desire to confide in Martha having instantly evaporated. By the time I've made the tea and brought two cups to the table, Martha's head has nodded forward and her eyes are closed, her breathing deep and steady.

I study her ring. The crystal-clear stones set in deep gold are breathtakingly beautiful. I'm suddenly aware I could so easily take it. She's a feeble old woman and I'm fit and strong.

I snap myself out of those thoughts. How could I even think about stealing from her? That's not my style at all. Instead, I go back to the sink and use the remaining hot water from the kettle to wash up the dishes. Then I sweep the floor and wipe down the cooker.

When I return to the table, I sit down opposite Martha, who is still fast asleep. My own eyes close as I take a sip. The tea is not very hot now, but I don't mind.

Warm, sweet tea. Just like Mum used to make it. Me and Mum. Drinking tea together while the birds sing cheerfully outside.

'Are you on your way home, dear?'

I jump and almost spill my tea. I open my eyes. Martha is staring at me.

'No!' My voice is sharp. Home? That tiny room where I sleep isn't 'home'.

'Sorry, dear. I didn't mean to startle you.'

I force a smile.

'I'm on my way to work. I always go to Luigi's on Fridays. It's my treat.' I glance at my watch. Quarter to six.

'Oh, no.' I stand up, pushing the chair back, grating it against the stone floor. 'I must run. I'm going to be late.'

'Where do you work?'

'In that big office block in the centre of town.' I've never told anyone before. It is hardly the best place and I'm not proud of it. I don't want Martha to know what my job really is. I fetch my coat and hug it around me although it is still rather soggy. 'I work six till ten every evening.'

'I see.'

I begin edging away.

'How old are you, dear?'

'Sixteen.'

'Ah.'

'Will you be all right now?' I ask. I want to get away before Martha asks any more questions.

'Yes, thank you, dear. I'm fine. I'm going to write a letter when you've gone.' Martha's hand delves into her handbag. The hand emerges. Her fist is clenched. She reaches out towards me. 'Here.'

I feel that electric current again as my hand meets

17

Martha's for a second. Then I fold my fingers round a crisp note that passes between us. I mutter my thanks and rush away along the corridor, confused, embarrassed, ashamed that I had, however fleetingly, contemplated stealing from her. As I reach the hall, I open my hand. A twenty-pound note. Then I feel the sharp eyes of Corvus, the raven, on me. I thrust the money into my pocket, open the door and stumble out into the darkness of the porch, slamming the door behind me.

Using the glow of the street light to guide me, I trot along the path to the gate. The black cat is sitting there, watching me, as if making sure I leave the premises. Then I run swiftly through the dark streets, watching my shadow in flight as it stretches and fades after each lamppost.

3

'This isn't good enough, Ella.' Hazel's shrill voice cuts through the dreary hum of the electric floor cleaner as I arrive, panting, inside the main entrance. There is a click and the hum dies away. 'You're five minutes late.'

I wince at the harshness of her voice that echoes around the empty lobby. Hazel is standing in front of the lifts. She steps away from the cleaner and places her hands firmly on her hips.

I can't help smirking as I wait by the door for a moment to get my breath back. Hazel's bleached mop of hair and her plump body in its luminous pink overall reflect upside-down in the shiny mock-marble floor. It makes me think of an overweight flamingo standing in a pool of custard.

'It's not funny!' snaps Hazel.

'I'm sorry,' I mutter. That's a lie. I'm not sorry at all. Who does Hazel think she is, anyway? She's only a lowly supervisor in a grotty job in an even grottier building.

'That's fifteen minutes docked from your pay.'

I bite my lip to stop the temptation to answer back. Fifteen minutes' pay is peanuts compared to the twenty pounds I've just 'earned' from Martha. My hand travels to my jeans pocket and pushes the note further down. I don't want to lose it.

'If it happens again, you'll have to go,' Hazel nags. 'If *I* can get here on time I can't see why you can't.'

Muttering under my breath, I amble across the lobby with my chin held high.

'Oh – *now* look at those footprints on my nice clean floor.'

I turn my head to look.

A line of footprints in wet sand. A hot, sunny day at the beach. The smell of seaweed; taste of salt on my lips; seagulls wheeling and squealing overhead. We've built a sandcastle almost as big as me. I'm jumping up and down, yelling, pointing at the sea. The tide is coming in. Dad is building a wall to try and stop the sea. Mum and I are laughing. We run into the waves, leaping and splashing.

The waves push forward and retreat, each wave coming a little bit nearer to our castle. I want the castle to last for ever, but soon it's surrounded. It

*collapses and is washed away, leaving nothing but a
misshapen mound of sand.*

   Washed away, like all my dreams.

'Don't you forget who gave you this job,' Hazel snaps. I feel
her disapproving grey eyes following me. 'You've got no
references. I could have sent you packing then and I can just as
easily do that now.'

   'Yes, Hazel.' I hate having to admit it, but I can't deny
the truth. Four weeks ago, when I fled from my home in
Barnfield, I'd been desperate for a job, *any* job, even one as
disgusting as this.

   'Turning up like that … if that other girl hadn't left me
in the lurch … '

   I shut out the cutting voice as I reach the far side of the
lobby. Pushing through the swing doors, I step into the
stairwell and open the door of the store cupboard. Trading my
coat for a pale green overall, I pull out the mop and bucket,
the disinfectant and loo brush, sprays, cloths and rubber gloves,
and head up the stairs.

   Rose, my fellow cleaner, is on the first-floor landing, her
grey hair tied up in a bright flowery headscarf. She beams at
me.

   'She been on at you again?' she asks.

   I nod. 'Threatened me with the sack!'

   'Yeah?'

   'Yeah, just because I was five minutes late.'

   I stop at the ladies' toilets and push the door open with

my bottom. The bucket clangs as I let it drop. 'This place stinks – in more ways than one!'

'Got to earn money somehow.'

I nod. 'And Madam Hazel's got no idea. I *am* well qualified for this job. My ghastly step-mother treated me like a slave!'

'Ah well,' says Rose as she walks away. 'Keep your chin up.'

I pull on the rubber gloves and move through the row of cubicles, scrubbing hard, working off my frustration. As I clean the washbasins and mop the floor, I begin to feel calmer.

Was that meeting with Martha really meant to happen? Is it possible that she could really make a difference to my life? Was that feeling of magic real – or only a figment of my imagination?

I'd like to visit her again. But the thought of that makes my stomach somersault. What excuse would I have to go there? It was so easy the first time, picking Martha up and taking her home. Then it seemed almost natural for her to invite me in. But it would be a different matter plucking up courage to go back. Would she be pleased to see me again?

Standing in front of the mirror, I reach in my pocket and pull out the purple note. I lift it close to my face.

'I hope you're the first of many,' I whisper. 'I'm going to save you, hide you away where the others won't find you. Not that Bea or Tilly need you. They've got fifty-pound notes coming out of their backsides! Rich daddies, mansions to live in at home, Olympic-size swimming pools in the garden. And I'm sure Velcro's too nice to even dream of pinching anything. But … '

I carefully fold the money, tuck it back into the pocket and gather the cleaning equipment together.

Friday night. I sigh. Everyone else must be out enjoying themselves while I'm stuck in here. Not for a second longer than I have to, though. I keep an eye on my watch as I scrub and polish away. I want to be ready to leave on the dot of ten.

At two minutes to ten, I hurry down the stairs. Exactly on the hour, I leave the equipment in the cupboard under the stairwell, strip off my overall, swap it for my coat and close the door. The swing doors fly open and Hazel blocks my exit.

'Well?' Although I'd expected her voice to bring me to a halt, as it does every evening as I'm about to leave, it still makes me jump.

'All done, Hazel,' I say, keeping my voice calm.

'Clean enough to eat your dinner off?'

'Yes.' I clench my fist and dig my nails into my palms to stop the urge to say something I'll regret.

'I'll check, of course,' Hazel snaps. 'If I find they're not up to standard … '

I feel like exploding. This woman is so infuriating! I grab the pay packet that is pushed roughly into my hand. Then I squeeze past her and speed across the shiny floor to the main entrance, without leaving the ghost of a footprint anywhere.

The night air strikes cold on my cheeks as I begin to sprint along the High Street. Suddenly, I skid and almost fall. The pavements are treacherous. Ice has formed on the puddles while I was working.

Treading more carefully, I reach Bella Casa café on a corner. It's a much bigger place than Luigi's and it's always lively in there on a Friday night. I can hear music and laughter from inside. I stop outside for a moment to watch and listen. My breath billows out in clouds of white mist as I stamp my feet and pull my coat sleeves down over my hands, trying to avoid freezing to death. Frost crystals have formed on the roofs and windows of the parked cars.

Just as I'm setting off again, the café door is flung open. Four lads rush out, talking loudly and laughing. I gawp and feel my blood pumping faster through my body, bringing a tingling sensation to my fingers. One of them is the best-looking boy I've ever seen. That tanned face and those gorgeous deep brown eyes. His golden hair shines like a halo in the bright beam of the café lights.

My heart is fluttering like butterfly wings. What's the matter with me? I'm not normally struck down at first sight by attractive males! Perhaps my life is changing in more ways than one. Maybe Martha has done this to me. Maybe she has more power than I'd ever have guessed.

'See you tomorrow at the rugby ground,' he calls, as they all set off in different directions. 'Ten o'clock?'

The sound of his voice bowls me over. So gravelly, like a pop star.

'See you, Finn!' someone calls.

'Finn,' I whisper, as I began to follow him. 'Yes. I like it.'

I feel a draw, like a magnet, and I'm unable to resist my wish to find out more about him. I wonder what makes me begin to tail him. All I know is I have this idea that goes round and round in my head and won't go away: 'Finn, you're the one for me.'

Friday 12th November
Madebury

Dear Cecily
Oh dear! I'm afraid I'm becoming quite unsteady on my pins. I must remember to carry my stick with me next time I come to see you. After I got off the bus on my way home, I fell over again, you see, right there in the High Street. If it weren't for a girl picking me up, I don't know how I would have got home.

Ella, she said her name was. A strange girl, gaunt, sad. I think she must be going through some kind of crisis. I can't make out what the problem is, but she fascinates me. I wouldn't say she is homeless, but I'm sure she doesn't live at home. I wonder why. All I know is that something is unsettling her.

She was very cagey about her job. She wouldn't discuss it. Oh, I do hope it's nothing dishonest or dangerous. Mind you, she had an eye for mother's ring. At one point I thought she might be thinking of stealing it. But she didn't, even when I dozed off at the kitchen table. I suppose that's why I gave her money — as a thank you for picking me up off the street, and for not taking advantage of me.

Jack would be very angry with me if he knew I'd invited another total stranger into the house. But he doesn't know and I won't tell him yet. It's my secret. I know you'll keep it, too.

It seems to me that Ella is a poor lost soul. I'm sure she was about to confide in me, then changed her mind. I'm determined to help her. I might be decrepit, but I haven't lost my power. You will tell me I am too mischievous, but I have to confess I have cast a little spell upon her. I hope it will work and have a happy outcome for her. I have a strong feeling I shall see her again very soon.

Your loving sister
Martha

4

Even though the pavements are so slippery, I'm forced to jog to keep up with Finn's pace. He strides ahead, up a steep hill away from the town centre, his arms swinging loosely at his sides. He has a sort of loping movement, foot-sure, graceful as a gazelle.

I stay in the shadows, not following too closely in case he turns round and sees me. That would be a disaster. I've never done anything like this before. I can't explain what's happened to me, unless it's something to do with Martha and the weird sensation of magic that came from her. All I know is I can't control this sudden urge to follow him.

Finn turns left. When I reach the corner and peer along the dark road, there is no sign of him. For a moment, I panic. Panting and slithering, I rush to the next corner and catch sight of him as he passes under a street lamp. But he is such a long way ahead, approaching a bend in the narrow road, a mere shadow now. I'm becoming desperate. I can't keep up. The cold air must have sapped my energy.

I lean on a fence, biting my lip to stop the tears of frustration. Everywhere is so dark, so unfamiliar. The streets are like a maze. I have no idea where I am. Four weeks is not long to get to know a town and so far I've only explored a fraction of Madebury. I've been following Finn blindly, not thinking about getting lost or about what I'd do when he reaches his house, if that is where he's going.

A noise behind me makes me jump. I whip round and peer into the darkness.

'Who's there?' I whisper.

The street is so quiet, so isolated. Would anyone hear me if I screamed? Would Finn hear? I shudder, trying to convince myself that it was nothing, probably a cat prowling in the garden behind the fence.

I make myself move, and turning my head to watch Finn again, I am just in time to see him disappear into a drive. It's the spur I need; it gives me the energy to carry on. I run straight down the middle of the road and arrive at a gateway as Finn reaches a house, set well back from the road. A security light reveals a large, modern detached house with a heavy wooden front door. Lights shine from several windows.

The gates have been left open. I creep onto the drive. Ducking down and keeping in the shadows, I skirt round a wide lawn and stop behind a large bush. Peering through the branches, I can see right into the downstairs rooms. I stare for a moment at the leather furniture, the large pictures on the walls, a china cabinet full of glinting crystal glasses. I can hear rock music playing.

'Hi, Mum!' Finn calls as he steps inside. 'I'm home.'

That is all I need to hear. This is where he lives, in this large house with a long drive and bright security lights. His family must be rich! I wait until I hear the click of the door closing and retrace my steps across the grass to the gateway. It's then that I notice the nameplate on the gate … *Falcon Ridge*.

I trot back along the lane, eyes alert for strangers, but see no one. At the corner I read the road name … *Kestrel Rise*. I can't help the sad smile. Mum would have loved these names, just as she had loved the birds themselves.

It isn't as difficult as I'd anticipated finding my way back to the town centre. I memorise the street names as I go. I want to be able to find my way back here in daylight. I feel upbeat, more confident. I've been bewitched, bowled over by Finn. I've found out where he lives and know where he is going in the morning. My hands and feet are frozen, but I'm not finished yet. There is one more thing I want to do before I go back to my lodgings.

The High Street is busy as people pour out of the cafés, pubs and restaurants. I feel safer in a crowd. That scary moment by the fence gave me the jitters. Normally, I don't mind the dark; I've been used to walking the streets alone at night when I lived in Barnfield with Dad and that woman. Anything to get away from the house and burn off my anger and hate.

I hurry past the office building with its storeys of unfriendly, faceless glass, all in darkness now. I wonder how much longer I'll be able to stand working there.

I side-step as two girls jostle against me. They giggle and stagger slightly. I wish I could be like them; relaxed and happy. I'd love someone to share my secrets and wishes, but I had to leave my mates behind when I ran away. Apart from the quick note I left for Dad, I've cut all ties. That way, no one can find me.

By the time I pass Luigi's café and reach the corner of Martha's road, I've begun to wonder whether this long trek has been a good idea. My hands and lips are chapped by the frost and biting wind, and I'm sure I've got blisters on the backs of both my heels where my shoes rub. And I feel so tired. The burst of energy that kicked in when Finn reached his house has slowly drained away.

'I might as well take a quick look, now I've got this far,' I mutter as I turn the corner.

The street looks the same as it did a few hours ago except that it's much darker now, and I tense up again. A sudden movement makes me swivel round, only to find I'm frightened by my own shadow. I almost turn back as a strange moaning sound echoes along the street, but it's just the wind blowing through the bare branches of the trees. I shut out the sound and walk towards Martha's house, keeping my eyes on the path ahead.

Frozen leaves crunch underfoot. Soon, I reach the gate and peer through. The same sightless windows. The black cat sitting in the shadows. The same air of mystery. I can't explain the magnetic pull of the house as I walk on, past an old brick wall. Then I stop at double gates I hadn't noticed the first time I was here. Parked inside the gates, up near to the house, there is a low, soft-topped sports car. Does Martha drive? Even if she does, I can't imagine this is her style. So whose is it?

5

The music swirls around my head.

Loud, louder. Fast, faster.

Exciting, invigorating, exhilarating.

My head twists and turns with the waves of sound. My limbs move magically in time to the rhythm. I sway and gyrate, totally taken over, lost in a dizzy, musical world.

My eyes are closed, but through my eyelids I can still see the flickering colours of the disco lights.

Fluttering feathers of a scarlet macaw ... red, blue, yellow, red ...

Mixing, mingling, merging into one brilliant white light.

A spotlight? On me?

People brush against me as they pass. I reach out to touch them, but they are not there. My eyes open. I'm alone.

Silence.

I'm in a room. Vast and shiny. A bathroom? In an expensive hotel?

Mirrors on every side. Reflections of reflections of reflections, each one smaller as the pattern diminishes.

Reflections of a beautiful girl dressed in a black dress.

Strapless, skin-tight, sexy.

A million sequins that sparkle and glitter, rippling like fish scales as I move under a spotlight again.

Black hair piled elegantly on top of my head, a diamond clasp holding it in place.

Earrings and a necklace with patterns of diamonds that remind me of bird wings.

A blinding flash.

I'm being swirled round. In someone's arms.

Strong arms, holding me tight.

The music is slow and sensuous. I'm melting away.

I look up, searching for the face of my partner. But the face is in shadow. I can't tell who it is. The dance goes on and on. It will never end.

A vast shadow looms overhead.

I duck away. The arms let go. I feel myself falling.

'You're safe with me.'

I reach out. The voice is luring me. I must reach it, but there is nothing to hold on to.

'You're safe with me.'

The voice is much quieter. It's fading away. I can't hear it any more. It's gone. I can't bear it.

Don't go. Please, don't go!

6

I sit up, wide awake, my breathing loud and my pulse thumping in my head. I stare around the bedroom, trying to bring myself back into the real world. Grey light sifts through the thin material of the curtains into the dull little room. Plain beige carpet, plain beige walls.

The end of the dream comes back to me. It's like the other dreams I've been having lately. The sound of Mum's voice echoing around inside my brain.

Blinking back the tears, I force myself to think of the hypnotic music, the dance, the amazing black dress. I wonder who the mysterious dancer was and hope it was Finn. Perhaps the dream has been foretelling the future.

I yawn, feeling as if I haven't slept, although I'd managed to go straight off to sleep last night. It was just before midnight when I got back, creeping in like a thief, careful not to wake the others.

I glance at my watch. Eight o'clock. Two whole hours before I'll see Finn again. I want that time to fly by, but I need to make sure I will look my best.

What's the matter with me? Getting all heated-up over someone I've only ever seen once. I've become obsessed. Martha *must* have cast a spell on me!

Calming myself, I listen at my door. Light footsteps on the landing. A door closing. Someone is up. It must be Velcro. The other two never surface until at least eleven o'clock on a Saturday morning. I open the door a crack and peer along the dark landing towards the bathroom. The light isn't on, so it must be free.

Twenty minutes later, I'm showered and dressed in my favourite jeans and sweater. I head downstairs. Velcro is sitting at the breakfast bar, a mug in his hand. He grins and I smile back at him. I really like him. He's been so good to me since we met a month ago, outside the corner shop where I was looking at the cards advertising rooms to let.

'There's a room going in my house,' says the young man with freckly pale skin and sandy hair who comes to stand beside me.

I stare at him. Is he winding me up? Or making a pass at me?

'There's three of us. Me and the Snob Sisters.' He grins. 'Well, Tilly and Bea aren't sisters, but they are dreadful snobs.

I'm Velcro, by the way – not my real name, of course – because I always stick around!'

I smile. I can't help liking him. But can I trust him?

'We're all first-year students at the University,' he says. 'The small front bedroom's free. Dave left last week.'

'I haven't got much money.'

'Don't worry. The house belongs to Tilly's dad. We don't pay a lot of rent.'

I know all the rules about safety, but I'm tempted. How can I tell if he's telling the truth?

'I'll think about it,' I say.

'Don't think for too long. You won't find another room quite so easily.'

At that moment, the shop door opens and a middle-aged woman comes out. She is wearing flat lace-up shoes and an anorak. She stops when she sees Velcro.

'Hello, love,' she says. 'Found anyone to fill that room yet?'

He shakes his head then turns to me. 'Hilda lives next door, don't you, Hilda?'

'Yes. You a friend of our Velcro, love?' she asks me.

'Not yet,' I say, my mind made up. 'But I'm taking the room, so I will be soon.'

'Great!' says Velcro.

'Wise choice,' says Hilda.

I follow them to a row of terraced houses. Hilda goes into the third house and Velcro points to the fourth. It's perfect.

'You were late in last night.' Velcro's voice brings me back.

'Sorry, I tried to be as quiet as I could. Did I wake you up?'

Velcro shakes his head. 'I wasn't asleep. I was wondering where you were. You took a long time coming home from work.'

I stand close to him, my hand on the table.

His hand closes over mine. 'I was worried.'

'Worried?' I raise my eyebrows.

Suddenly, I notice a blush spreading up Velcro's face right into his scalp, under the thinning sandy hair. I slide my hand from under his and walk to the sink to fill the kettle. Standing with my back to him, I take a deep breath to recover from the surprise. Does Velcro fancy me? I hope not. He's just a nice guy who has been my ally since I came here. A balance against the other two. Someone to talk to. No more.

I plug in the kettle, trying to act as if I hadn't noticed his blush.

'I was just wandering the streets,' I say. 'Finding my way around town.'

'In the dark?'

I'd been going to tell him about Finn, but now that is out of the question.

'I needed to think – try and sort my brain out.' I turn round. His face has returned to its normal pallor. 'I met an old woman yesterday,' I say, keeping my voice flat. 'She fell down right there outside Luigi's. I picked her up off the pavement and took her home.'

'That was nice of you.'

'Maybe.' I don't tell him about the money, which I've tucked inside an old shoe at the bottom of my wardrobe. Or about her strange power.

'Ella ... ' Velcro is fidgeting. 'What are you doing today? I ... I wondered if you'd ... like to ... go for a coke?'

I occupy my hands by rattling spoons in the drawer and putting coffee granules in my mug, but my mind is buzzing. Is he coming on to me? In silence, I wait for the kettle to boil. I don't want to hurt his feelings, but now seems like a good time to establish some ground rules. I pour the hot water into the mug, then pick it up, take a deep breath and turn to face him again.

'Look.' I'm finding it difficult to say the right words. 'You're a lovely guy and I'm very fond of you, but can we keep it at that?'

He forces a laugh. 'Yeah, course we can. I wasn't ... I mean ... don't get me wrong ... just a drink ... not a date or anything.'

I shrug and smile, hoping I'm not raising his hopes. 'OK ... you're on. I've got things to do this morning, but I'll meet you at about eleven-thirty.' What harm can it do? 'Where?'

'How about Bella Casa?'

Coffee slops onto the floor as I almost drop the mug. Bella Casa? It's where I saw Finn last night! Supposing he goes there with his friends after rugby?

Velcro rushes to the sink and fetches a cloth.

'Sorry, don't you like Bella Casa?'

'Er ... no ... yes ... I ... ' Then I think about it. If Finn did come into the café it would give me another chance to be near him. 'No problem … Bella Casa it is. Eleven-thirty. See you there.'

Carrying my mug in shaky hands, I hurry from the kitchen, wondering if I've made a mistake, hoping Velcro is not expecting anything to come of it.

Back in my room, I look at my watch. I gasp. I've taken too long talking to Velcro. Leaving the hot coffee on the window sill, I brush my hair and do my make-up. Then, satisfied with my appearance, I slurp down some of the coffee, put on my coat and trainers, wrap a scarf round my neck and head out of the house.

Although the frost has melted it's still bitterly cold as I walk towards the town centre. Last night, I'd been sure about going to the rugby field, but suddenly I feel nervous. I know it isn't a good idea, but I still keep going, as if drawn by some invisible force towards him.

When I reach the High Street, the pavement is crowded with people carrying bags bulging with early Christmas shopping. Shoulders hunched and head down, I weave between them.

Suddenly, I side-step to avoid a wide pushchair and find myself jammed against the wooden frame of a brightly-lit shop window. Raising my eyes, I glance inside. My stomach lurches and I reach out to clutch at the window frame. It isn't possible! I blink several times, to clear my vision. But I'm not mistaken. There, in the centre of the display, is a black dress.

Strapless, skin tight, sexy. A million sequins that

sparkle and glitter, rippling like fish scales as I move under a spotlight again.

The dress of my dream!

7

The café is heaving with people when I push in through the door. At first I think Velcro isn't there. Then I catch a glimpse of his pale face at the far end of the room. He's managed to bag a table. I wave and squeeze between tables and chairs, shopping bags and pushchairs. I reach him at last.

'Coke?' he asks, above the chatter. 'I'm buying, remember.'

'Cappuccino, please.' I don't tell him I'm frozen to the bone again after standing on the touchline in a muddy field. I'm hoping a cappuccino will warm me up. He goes to the counter and returns with two steaming cups.

'You look like an iceberg.' He puts the cups down on the table. 'Where've you been?'

'Oh, nowhere, really. Just out and about.'

'Finding your way round town again?' He's staring right into my eyes as if he doesn't believe me. 'You're being very mysterious, Ella. Anything you want to talk about?'

'No … thanks … really … ' I take a sip of my drink and feel the warmth spread down my throat. 'It's just … '

There are very few people on the touchline. This turns out to be only a practice so it isn't very exciting and I feel rather conspicuous. But I stay for a while, stamping my feet and rubbing my hands together as the ball passes up and down the field. I definitely have a reason to stay. Finn!

I know I'll probably 'catch my death' as Gran used to say, but the sight of Finn bowls me over. He looks twice as gorgeous in shorts and rugby shirt. Just looking at him makes my heart flutter! I can tell he's the best player there. Several times, he runs past me. I wonder if he's noticed me.

The stunning image of the dress flashes in front of me. I feel unnerved by it. It's uncanny, terrifyingly so. An exact copy of the one in my dream. How can that happen? Martha's magic? People don't have that kind of magic … do they?

But the dress is beautiful! It's second on my list of wants – after Finn.

'It's just what?' Velcro is leaning forward.

'Sorry,' I say. 'I'm always doing this … I'm a bit of a dreamer … What were we saying? Oh yes … I was just watching rugby, if you must know.'

Velcro says something else, but I don't hear. The door has opened. I'm staring over his shoulder at the boys who have just entered the café. In the midst of them all, laughing and joking, is Finn. I watch him weave his way to the counter, chatting to people as he passes them. Everyone grins or laughs or speaks to him.

'Is that why you're not listening to me, Ella?' I feel Velcro's hand on my arm. He's turned his head to watch Finn, too. 'So that's the competition, eh?'

'Not competition!' I snap. 'You know what I said this morning.'

Velcro sighs. What a contrast to Finn! He sounds pathetic. And how can he be in love with me already? I've only known him such a short while. Then I smile to myself. I fancied Finn after only less than one minute! Perhaps I shouldn't be so harsh on poor Velcro.

'Sorry,' I mutter.

He doesn't reply. I pick up my cup and take a large sip. I wish now that I hadn't agreed to come here, even though it has given me another chance to see Finn. But this isn't the way to get to know him.

'Shall we go?' I drain my cup and feel the liquid warm my throat. 'We could walk the long way home, if you like.'

'OK.' Velcro sounds like he doesn't care. He quickly finishes his coffee and stands up. As we head for the door, I glance towards Finn. He's leaning on the counter, his head flung back, laughing loudly.

Let's face it, I think as I push open the door and walk out into the cold air, he could have absolutely anyone. Why could I ever imagine he would be interested in me … unless Martha's magic will reach him, too?

Velcro and I walk in silence for a while and soon I begin to feel more comfortable beside him. I sense him relax, and that cheers me up. I really don't want to lose him as a friend.

'That old lady,' I say at last. 'Martha. Do you think I should go and see her again?'

'Why not? She's probably lonely.'

'That's what I thought.' I'm ashamed to admit I can't help hoping I might get some more money. How else am I going to afford that dress?

'Is she rich?'

I stare at Velcro. Has he read my mind?

'Well,' I say, trying to sound innocent. 'She lives in a big old house, so I suppose she probably is.'

Velcro grins. 'All the more reason to get in her good books!'

I speed up and walk a few paces ahead of him. It's weird. How could he be so right about me? He catches me up.

'Sorry, I was only joking.'

When we arrive home, Bea and Tilly are buzzing around the kitchen like demented wasps. They ignore Velcro and me.

'Oh, what can I wear?' wails Bea. 'All my dresses are at least a month old.'

'So are mine. I'll have to ask Daddy to buy me a new one.'

'Same here. My pa always lets me have what I want.'

I feel like throwing up. These two spoilt brats live in a different world.

'Shall we go for long dresses?'

'Backless?'

'Or strapless?'

'What colour?'

The questions and chatter go on and on. I try to shut my ears to them as I make a sandwich from the little store on my shelf in the fridge. I wonder what they are so excited about. I don't really care, but from the way they keep on about it and keep glancing in my direction I know the Snob Sisters are dying to tell.

'So what's this all about?' I ask.

Tilly gives me a stare fit for a worm under her shoe. 'I suppose we might as well tell you, though I don't know why we should.'

'Please yourself.' I really don't want to know.

'Not that you'd ever have a chance of going,' says Bea with a superior smirk. 'It's a party!'

'So?' Velcro is grinning. 'You're always going to parties.'

'Yes, but this one's a bit special,' says Bea.

'Absolutely everyone's going.'

'It's going to be fantastic.'

'When?'

'11th December. Only a few weeks to get kitted out.'

As I bite into my sandwich, I blank out the incessant prattle of the Snob Sisters. I don't care about the party. Velcro is right. The girls are always off to some do or other.

But their talk of dresses brings my dream back to me.

The dress. Dancing in his arms. Just supposing Finn is going to be there ...

I'd really love that dress.

There must be a way of getting it, apart from stealing it or Martha giving me more money.

I might ask Dad. Perhaps it's time I got back in touch with him.

I sigh and bite my lip. I miss Dad terribly. I'll have to psyche myself up to ring him.

Later.

First, I'll go and see Martha.

Tomorrow.

I wonder how she is after her fall.

8

Monday, three o'clock. Plenty of time. Three hours before I'm due at work. And I want to arrive at the house in daylight.

I hurry past Luigi's café and on towards Martha's road, but when I reach the corner I hesitate. Do I need to visit her again? Will she be pleased to see me?

I walk along slowly, burying my nose in the bunch of chrysanthemums I've just picked from the garden. I keep trying to work out my motives. I've discussed it with Velcro and gone over it so many times in my mind, but I still can't decide why I'm going.

Three days have passed since I met Martha. Three days since she slipped me that twenty-pound note. Is that my reason for going again? Or do I need to check that she is all right after her fall? Or is it that crazy feeling that these magical powers she seems to have might change my life? Strange things have certainly happened since then, especially my sudden infatuation with Finn!

I keep going. The worst thing that could happen would be Martha refusing to see me. Anyway, I know I can easily walk right by the house if I lose my nerve at the last minute.

As I reach the lamppost outside the house, a white feather drifts past my face and lightly brushes my cheek. I stop and glance up, expecting to see a big white bird perched on the lamppost or flying overhead, but there is nothing. Just the stark tree branches and a dull grey wintry sky. Fascinated, I watch the feather as it dances in slow motion, floating on currents of air, buffeted from time to time by a light breeze. Slightly concave, it rocks gently as if cocooning a young precious child.

I'm that child, wrapped in a white lacy shawl, cradled in Mum's arms. There's a contented smile on Mum's face, as if her happiness will last forever.

I blink and push the image of that photo to the back of my mind. Amazingly, the feather is still floating just above the soggy leaves on the pavement. I bend down and cup it in my hand before it reaches the ground.

Cradling the feather, I open the gate and stride up the path, my eyes fixed firmly on Martha's front door. I climb the steps into the porch. It doesn't seem as sinister in daylight as it did in the darkness of Friday afternoon, but I have to steel myself to knock.

The sound of the door knocker echoing inside the house makes my stomach tighten and I'm tempted to run away. But I stick at it. While I wait, I try to remember what the hall looks like. My memory is rather hazy. I had been concentrating too hard on Martha to take everything in. I remember the musty smell. And there is one thing I'll never forget. The raven.

I knock again. Nothing. Perhaps Martha is out. Perhaps she has seen me coming and decided not to answer the door. Maybe she can't come to the door. I hope she hasn't fallen again. I shuffle my feet on the stone floor, suddenly realising how anxious I've become about her.

Bending down, I peer through the letterbox. I listen. There is a distant sound, faint and high-pitched. It's Martha's voice.

'Please wait. I'm coming.'

I release the letterbox and stand back, feeling guilty, like an intruder. A few moments later, I hear the click of a key being turned in the lock. Slowly, the door swings open and Martha stands peering out at me. She smiles as she takes the flowers I thrust at her.

'Hello, dear.' Her voice is welcoming and her eyes twinkle. 'I'm so glad you've come. I've been quite worried about you.'

She stands back to let me step into the hall.

'Hello, Martha.' I feel the feather tickling my palm as I smile back at her. 'I've been worried about you, too.'

As before, I have the sensation that I'm being watched, but this time it doesn't unnerve me. As I turn my head and stare into the bead-like eyes of Corvus, I can't help noticing how his sleek black plumage contrasts so starkly with the white feather in my hand.

I slip the feather into my pocket as I follow Martha through to the kitchen. Although she moves slowly, she seems steadier and more confident than on Friday.

The kettle is boiling madly on the range.

'Tea?' I ask. 'You sit down. I'll make it.'

I'm almost at the cooker when I stop. Martha must think badly of me for waltzing straight in and taking over.

'Sorry,' I say. 'It's … I used to make tea for someone, that's all.'

Mum is reclining on the lounger in the garden. She looks so pale, her eyes sunk in deep pools of shadow. I bring her a cup of tea and we sit together chatting. I try to keep cheerful for Mum's sake. Look! There's a bird in the tree. What is it? I run in for the binoculars and we take turns to watch it until it flies away. A brown feather wafts down on the breeze and lands gently in Mum's hands.

I fight back the tears. If only I could make Mum better.

Martha sits down at the table.

'Do you want to talk about it, dear? Would that help?'

I make the tea while I think about it. I've never been able to talk about Mum since she died, not even with Dad. And when that counsellor visited the house, I refused. Everything was too painful then. But am I ready now?

'I … I miss … ' I begin. My shaking hands make the cups rattle as I put them down on the table. 'I … '

'Who do you miss, dear?' Martha's old, gnarled hand close over mine.

'My … mum.' As soon as the words are out of my mouth, I feel my eyes fill with tears. There is nothing I can do to stop them flowing. I reach in my pocket for a tissue and wipe my eyes.

Martha stays quite still.

'I guessed as much,' she says. 'How long ago did she … pass away?'

I swallow. 'Six months.' It's incredible. I remember it like it was yesterday, yet those six months seem more like six centuries. Six centuries of nightmare!

'I noticed you had a feather in your hand when you came in, dear.'

I nod, feeling tears welling up again. 'It reminded me of Mum. She loved birds.'

'And you shared that love?'

'Mmm. She took me bird watching. I miss that, too.'

'Of course you do, dear.'

Martha picks up her cup and sips her tea. She closes her eyes and sighs.

'Lovely,' she murmurs. 'Just how I like it.'

I sip mine too, feeling better for having opened up some of my past with Martha.

Suddenly, I feel that ripple of excitement again. It shoots through my body like a bolt of electricity and makes me tingle all over. Is it the tea? How can Martha have such a strong effect on me?

The moment over, I finish my drink then I look at Martha and smile. She's fallen asleep again, this time with her cup still in her hand. I carefully take it then tiptoe away from the table and quietly set to work. I wash up, clean the cooker, sweep the kitchen floor and tidy a few papers on the dresser in the corner.

After a little while, Martha wakes with a start.

'Oh, sorry, dear,' she says, blinking at me. 'I must have nodded off.' She looks across at the draining board. 'And you've done my washing up again. Thank you. You're so kind.'

As I leave the house, I skip down the steps and trot to the gate, whistling softly to myself. The cat meanders between my legs while I stop to open the gate. I bend to stroke it then hurry away along the road, some of my questions answered.

I now know for certain that I went to Martha's house a second time to see how she was; not in the hope of getting more money. I think she was pleased to see me again. Somehow, I think she was expecting me. I can't quite explain to myself what it is about her, but I'm absolutely sure that she's using magic powers to help me. What I can't understand is, why? Maybe I'll find out next time.

I stop as I reach the dress shop. The black dress is still in the window. I sigh. There must be other ways of getting money for it. Perhaps I could get some overtime at work, or find another job for during the daytime.

It's definitely time I rung Dad.

9

'Hello?'

His voice sounds hoarse and tired.

'Dad?'

'Ella?' He lowers his voice to a whisper. 'Where are you?'

'I'm ... '

'Who's that?' A harsh, high-pitched squawk cuts in. It's *her*.

'Oh, er ... nobody, darling ... wrong number.'

'Dad?'

The phone has gone dead, its loud purring deafening me. I snatch the receiver away from my ear and slam it down. I'll never get to talk to him while that creature is around. From the moment she took over our lives, she made sure I was wiped off the face of his earth. Mum's so-called friend. She'd been watching and waiting for Mum to die.

I leave the phone box in a daze. A few minutes later, I find myself in the park, sitting on a bench, staring at the pond, my mind thousands of miles away.

Hot, dry, golden grasslands. Beautiful golden lions hunting, devouring their prey.

> *Circle of life, Mum says, like in* The Lion King.
> *I smile, but not for long.*

A shadow blocks out the sun. We shiver. A black and white vulture has landed on top of a nearby tree. Shoulders hunched, its hooded eyes are watching and waiting. When the lions leave, this ugly bird will peck off every last morsel of flesh till there's nothing left.

That's what *she* has done to Dad. Watched and waited. And now she's pecking off every last morsel of his flesh.

I leap to my feet. I've been so lost in my daydream, I'm going to be late for work again if I don't run like a hare.

Breaking all records, I make it on time. I'm not giving Hazel the satisfaction of gloating over me again, or an excuse to sack me.

While I work, my brain is in overdrive, flitting

between Martha and Dad, my evil step-mother, Finn, and that dress. I'm still hyper-brain-active when I leave on the dot of ten.

I stand outside Bella Casa for a few moments, peering through the steamed-up glass, but Finn isn't inside.

Anyway, there is something else I've decided to do. Cursing my luck that someone pinched my mobile just after I left home, I head for the phone box again and dial. This time, I'll keep Dad talking; make sure he doesn't ring off.

'Good evening.'

My stomach does a dive. The sweet drooling voice is a shock. I hold my breath and say nothing. I can't ask for Dad when I know very well that she'll refuse to let me speak to him. Anyway, I don't want her to know I've been in touch.

'Hello?' A sharp edge has pushed its way into her voice. 'Who is this?'

I can't move let alone speak.

'Ella, is that you?'

I gasp.

'If it is, listen to me and listen well. Keep out of our lives. Do you hear me?'

I slam the receiver down again, only this time I do it with venom. I hate that woman with every cell of my body.

Tiredness washes over me like a tidal wave. I lean my forehead against the glass of the phone box, biting my lip hard. I refuse to let that woman make me cry. I'll never let her pick over my bones.

But I know she's already begun, by turning Dad against me, me against him, forcing herself into every corner of our lives where the memory of Mum is still so strong, attempting to erase all evidence that Mum ever existed.

Velcro is in the kitchen when I stagger in. He glances at my face and pulls out a chair from under the table. I sink into it, put my head on the table and close my eyes.

'That bad?'

I don't reply. I know he doesn't expect me to answer and I silently thank him for being so understanding.

I'd have stayed there all night if Bea and Tilly hadn't arrived home with their usual chatter about boys and parties and dresses. That gives me just enough energy to climb to my room and flop on the bed. I'm aware of Velcro hovering in the doorway for a moment, then he takes the hint and closes my door.

Tuesday 16th November
Madebury

Dear Cecily
　Thank you for replying so soon. I was right. That girl did call again, yesterday afternoon, but you don't need to worry. I knew I wasn't being foolish letting her in the house and giving her money. You warned me that it would have been easy for her to turn nasty and demand more, but she didn't. On the contrary, she did some housework while I had forty winks over my cup of tea.
　However, I didn't give her more money, just as you suggested. I didn't want her to expect it every time she came. I guess you doubt

if she'll come a third time, but I believe she won't be able to stop herself. Besides, I have an idea how I can help that happen. She already feels my power drawing her to me.

I was also right about her being a poor troubled soul. She has begun to confide in me. She cried, in fact. She misses her dead mother. There's more, I know there is, lots more, but I must be patient. She'll tell me when she's ready. She might have done if I hadn't fallen asleep at the crucial moment.

Your loving sister
Martha

10

There is no way I'll try and speak to Dad at home again, not with *her* always lurking nearby. I decide to ring him at the bank, but I keep putting it off. Several times, I go to the phone box on the corner of the High Street then chicken out, afraid he'll refuse to speak to me.

Eventually, I take a grip of myself and dial his number. After a few rings, there is a click.

'Hello. This is Mr Sharma's secretary. Can I help you?'

Brenda sounds so formal I almost put the receiver down. But I desperately want to speak to Dad and this is the only way. My whole body shakes as I begin.

'Can I speak to Mr Sharma, please?'

'Who is this?'

'Ella.'

'Oh, Ella, my love. So lovely to hear your voice. Are you OK?' Brenda gushes in the way I remember so well. It gives me the courage to carry on.

'Yes.'

'Your dad's been so worried about you.'

I feel heat rising in my face. How dare he say he's been worried when he's virtually ignored me over the past six months, thanks to the vulture! But I manage to control my anger. I don't want to start off on the wrong foot with Dad.

'Is he there?'

'Of course. I'll put you through.'

I wait for what seems like hours and almost put the receiver down and run. At last, he picks up the phone.

'Hello, Ella. Thanks goodness you've got in touch. The other evening … I … '

I'm shocked. He sounds so tired and old. Is it my fault or is the witch treating him even worse than before? I swallow hard.

'Hi, Dad. How are you?'

'Fine.'

Liar! He sounds about 85 years old, not 45.

'Where are you?' he asks.

'I'd rather not say.' Actually, I'm only about ten miles away from him, but I'm not letting on. 'Didn't you read my note when I left?'

'Yes, but … ' He clears his throat. 'You said you wouldn't be far away and I wasn't to try and find you. I rang Jodie. I hoped at least your best friend would know where you were. She said you were fine. I assumed she knew where you were.'

I silently thank Jodie for lying for me.

'You know why I had to do it, don't you, Dad?'

There is a long silence.

'So why are you ringing me now?' His voice has switched a gear. Suddenly, he sounds business-like and cold. I know I've struck a nerve.

'I need money.' I blurt it out. 'I've got a job, but it doesn't pay much and I can barely afford my room and ... '

The phone buzzes. Dead. I stare at the receiver. Dad has cut me off at the mention of money. I put the receiver down and slump against the side of the phone box, breathing deeply to calm myself. Then I redial.

The phone is engaged. I try several times, but I get no response. I presume Brenda has been told to keep the phone off the hook so I can't get through.

Muttering under my breath as I leave the phone box, I curse him and that woman who's taken control of his life.

11

The house is silent and in darkness, but the street lamps send their glow into the hallway. I go straight to the kitchen and press the light switch. The fluorescent strip flickers a few times then floods the room with brilliant light. As I fill the kettle I notice two identical envelopes on the counter. I switch the kettle on then peer at the envelopes, one addressed to Bea, the other to Tilly. I remember seeing them a few days ago and I know what's inside. The party invitations!

It wouldn't do any harm to peek at them. The Snob Sisters would never know.

I pick up Bea's envelope. Sliding my thumb and forefinger carefully under the flap, I pull out a single sheet of card. It's written in fancy lettering. I spot the date, which I already know, and the time, '8 till L8.'

Suddenly, my head spins. I grip the counter as strange sounds like the flurry of birds' wings fill my ears. I shake my head to clear my brain, refusing to believe what I've just read. One word has leapt out at me from the card. A name.

Finn. It's Finn's party. His eighteenth birthday. And he's invited Bea and Tilly. I've *got* to go now. Somehow!

The front door opens. Two giggling voices in the hall. With fluttery hands, I shove the invitation back into its envelope and put both envelopes back exactly where I found them. As Bea and Tilly reach the kitchen, I'm concentrating hard on making my coffee.

'Make me a cup, Ella,' says Tilly.

Her tone makes me grip my mug fiercely, but I don't retaliate.

'And me,' said Bea. 'Nice and strong.'

I dutifully obey and place two mugs on the table. They sit down and begin sipping the hot drink.

'Did you iron my blouse, Ella?' Bea asks.

I nod. 'I've hung it just outside your room.'

She turns her back on me and whispers in Tilly's ear. They both giggle. The next moment, Tilly is glaring at me.

'But you didn't clean this floor like I told you this morning, did you?' she says. 'Really! I let you have your room for a pathetically low rent. You don't want us to find someone else for your room … ?'

'No!' I feel like saying something rude, but I know I'm lucky that this rich kid charges me such a tiny rent for my room. I have to put up with being treated like a servant if I want to stay. 'I'll do it in the morning,' I mutter.

Normally, I would have gone straight to my room. I can't stand much more of them. But things have changed. I didn't manage to read where the party is going to be. I need to know.

'Daddy's sent me some money for a dress,' says Bea. 'I've seen one in that boutique in town.' She tosses her long blonde hair so it shimmers. 'It's red and strapless and very revealing. Do you think red would suit me, Ella?'

I stare, too surprised to answer. She's never asked my opinion about anything before.

'Well?'

'I … um, y-yes,' I stutter.

'Is that all?'

'You'll look stunning,' I say.

She gives me a hard look to see if I'm being sarcastic, but I mean it. I nod, to convince her.

'*Oo*, we have a new fashion advisor, do we?' Tilly's mouth turns up in a sneer. 'What about me, then, if you're such an expert?'

'I'm not … only Bea did ask me and I think her blonde hair … '

'I'm getting a silver dress, if you can call it a dress.' Tilly says. 'It's so short it'll barely cover my bum. And so low cut, Finn won't have to use his imagination … ' She sticks out her chest and pouts at me. 'So?'

I hate her. She can't have Finn.

I look at her bright copper curls and nod again. 'Silver will be perfect,' I say, lying through my teeth. 'With your hair and green eyes, you'll look fantastic.'

They ignore me for a while, drinking their coffee, and

giggling and chattering about people I don't know. I feel relieved. Neither of them is going to wear black to the party. If only I could afford to buy that dress!

'Where's the party?' I dare to ask.

'At the manor,' says Tilly.

'Manor?'

'Yes, you know. Critchley Manor. About a mile out of town.'

I nod. I've heard of it, though I have no idea where it is. But I'll make sure I find out.

'Can't wait,' says Tilly. 'I'm in with a chance there.'

'Oh, no.' It's Bea's turn to pout. 'Finn's mine.'

I have to feign ignorance, but I want to find out everything I can about Finn.

'Who's Finn?' I ask, my heart pounding. 'Is he *that* gorgeous?'

'*Is* he?' Eyes rolling, Tilly does a mock swoon.

'Is he at your uni?' I ask, keeping my voice even.

'No. He's a year younger than us. Got a place at uni next year, I think.'

'So how d'you know him?'

'Mummy and Daddy know his parents,' says Bea. 'So we've both met him a few times, haven't we, Tilly? I've been hoping for a chance to snog him for an absolute age.'

If only I could get to that party. But what chance would I stand against my two housemates? I don't need a mirror to show me the contrast between us.

And anyway, how *can* I go? I've got no money, no dress, no transport. And I'm not very good at gate-crashing.

I sigh and take the empty mugs they pass me to the sink and wash them up, like a good servant. But while I dry them up, I try to think of a plan. I'm determined to get there somehow.

12

'Hello. This is Mr Sharma's secretary. Can I help you?'

'Brenda. He cut me off and ... '

'Thank goodness you rang back, my love. He was worried you'd think that. I'll put you through again.'

I let out a rush of air as relief spreads through me. Dad didn't cut me off purposely. He *is* worried about me. He's willing to talk to me. And I realise my real reason for phoning him. Of course I need the money, but I want to talk to *him*, too.

'Ella!' Dad begins. 'I'm sorry. I don't know what happened yesterday. You were saying ... you need money ... You're not living on the streets are you?'

'No, Dad. Nothing like that. I've got a room in a house with three others.'

'And you've got a job?'

'Mmm.'

Dad is silent. I wonder what he's thinking; what he'll say about the money.

'Ella, why don't you let me know where you're living … ?'

'No!'

'Why are you being so secretive?'

'You must realise, Dad. It's … *her*.' I shudder. I can't bring myself to say my step-mother's name. It makes me feel sick.

'So you won't be coming home?'

'What do you think?'

There is a long pause. 'I see.'

'But … ' How can I admit that I'd like to see him; that I've missed him terribly, even after what he said before I left home?

'Well then,' he says. 'How about meeting up … somewhere else?'

My heart flutters like the lightest bird's wing. That's exactly what I'd hoped he'd say.

'OK.' I try to sound casual. I don't want him to think he has won me over too easily. There is only one way he could do that. Get rid of *her!* 'When?'

I hear rustling of paper as he works out when he can spare the time.

'Thursday? Are you free at lunchtime?'

My head spins as I take in what he's said. 'Er … Thursday lunchtime's fine,' I manage to say.

'Do you still like Chinese?'

'Mmm.'

'There's a Golden Panda in Fernton, near where I work.'

'Yeah. I know it.'

'Noon?'

'I'll be there.'

'Great. Bye, Ella.'

'Bye, Dad.'

I lean against the side of the phone box and close my eyes. I wonder if meeting Dad will make any difference at all. The last time I saw him he was so smitten with *her* that he couldn't see how much he was under her spell.

A sudden rap on the glass makes me jump. I open the door of the phone box.

'You gonna be in there all day?'

The young man in a filthy anorak and cap stands aside for me. I step round him, welcoming the cold air that cools my hot head.

Thursday. I can't wait to see Dad.

13

The board outside the newsagent is full of adverts. My eyes scour them eagerly. Maybe I'll find my ideal job – or at least somewhere I can earn extra money.

Copy typist … I can't type. Washer-up in a restaurant … I suppose I could do that, but it's evenings so that's out. Office cleaner … same hours I do already. Shop assistant … previous experience essential. More cleaners required. More dirty jobs in cafés. More boring jobs that pay a pittance.

I sigh as I turn away from the window. I'll look again tomorrow. But without references, I'll never get anything better.

I don't feel like going back to the house. Bea and Tilly will get up my nose if they are home, and I don't feel like confiding in Velcro. I find myself turning the corner into Martha's road. I pass her house. The double gates are closed and the flashy car isn't there. Perhaps I imagined seeing it. I turn back and push open Martha's front gate.

'Come in, dear.' Martha pulls the door open wide in answer to my knock. 'I was hoping I'd see you again.'

I smile, pleased that she is happy to see me.

Stepping into the hall, I nod at Corvus, just in case he is real after all, then follow Martha to the kitchen. Everything is exactly the same as before, as if time has stood still; the same old-fashioned range, a pile of dirty crocks on the draining board, the old lady sitting down at the table, me putting the kettle on and making tea.

'How are your knees?' I ask as we sip our tea.

'All healed, thanks to you, dear.' The warmth of her smile spreads right through me. I feel her magic again, taking me over and I'm more relaxed than I've been for ages. 'Do you want to talk, dear?' she asks.

I nod, but I don't know where to begin.

'Tell me about your childhood,' she says, so quietly I hardly hear. 'Were you happy then?'

I close my eyes and take a deep breath. I stand outside myself, looking in. I begin to speak.

The little child playing and laughing with Mum and Dad. Friends, adventures, holidays, always with Mum and Dad somewhere in the background. Bird watching with Mum, the ornithologist. Blue skies, sunshine, warmth. Then clouds, dark clouds. Mum changing, growing light as a feather, fading away.

When I open my eyes, Martha is watching me closely.

'Sorry,' I mutter, feeling myself blush. 'You didn't need to hear all that.'

'On the contrary, dear,' she says. 'I hope it was therapeutic.'

I don't know what that means, but I'm too embarrassed to ask. What I've told her has been drawn out of me as if I've been hypnotised. I feel I'm floating on air like a bird, with the sensation that some of the misery of my life has been magicked away. I take Martha's empty cup. Suddenly, she shivers.

'Are you cold?' I ask.

'A little chilly, dear. Would you mind fetching my cardigan? It's in the lounge.'

I hurry along the passage into the hall and stand face to face with Corvus.

'Where's the lounge?' I ask him.

His beady eyes seem to move towards a door in the opposite side of the hall.

'Thanks.' I can't help grinning. I must be off my head, speaking to a bird, and a stuffed one at that!

The door creaks as I push it open and I enter a room as old-fashioned as the kitchen. The dull green velvet curtains are half-closed, but I can make out a faded patterned carpet and four large brown armchairs. Valuable-looking ornaments stand on a huge white mantelpiece around the fireplace. Above the mantelpiece there is an oval mirror, and several paintings hang from the walls. A grandfather clock stands in a corner. It has stopped at three o'clock.

I begin looking for Martha's cardigan, but stop abruptly in the middle of the room, almost tripping over a pair of black trainers. I frown. I can't believe Martha is a secret marathon runner or netball player. And I can't imagine her going to the gym. I look more closely at the trainers. They are large, man-size, with white stripes down the sides. What is a pair of man's trainers doing here?

I sneeze and my chest feels tight. I realise everywhere is covered in a thick layer of dust. The room hasn't been cleaned for ages. Poor Martha probably has no strength for housework and whoever has left the trainers there hasn't bothered to do it. Spotting a grey cardigan on one of the armchairs, I snatch it up and hurry back to the kitchen, not wanting Martha to think I've been snooping. I needn't have worried. She's snoring gently with her head nodded onto her chest. I drape the cardigan around her shoulders and do the washing up. It's getting to be a habit.

I have time to think as I clean the dishes and plates and stack them on the draining board. Is there a man living here? If so, that would explain the trainers, the car and the extra things to wash. I wonder who he is.

14

I catch a bus to Fernton and find the Golden Panda restaurant easily. I'm ten minutes early. I want to watch him, see how he looks. I wonder if he'll be pleased to see me or whether he's as nervous as I am.

I stand in a doorway on the shady side of the street opposite the restaurant. I know which direction he'll come from. His bank is only a few minutes' walk away.

Suddenly, as the church clock begins to strike noon, there he is, hurrying towards me, dead on time. He looks like he sounded on the phone; old and tired. He's lost weight, got bags under his eyes and his hair is thinning. For a second, I can't help a strange feeling of satisfaction. Serves him right for marrying the vulture. Then I shudder. I hate her even more for making him suffer.

Without glancing round, Dad pushes the heavy glass door of the restaurant and goes inside. I count slowly up to twenty, breathing deeply on each number then walk to the door.

'Calm, stay calm,' I mutter under my breath as I follow him inside.

Adjusting my eyes to the dim light of the restaurant, I glance around. It seems quite smart with its red flock wallpaper and white cotton tablecloths. The place is half-full and everyone is well-dressed, making me glad I'd decided to wear a skirt instead of my usual jeans. A waiter has just seated Dad at a table in an alcove. At that moment, he looks up. I freeze under his gaze like a terrified animal in headlights.

'Would you like a table?'

The question makes me jump. I turn to the waiter at my side.

'Oh, er, no, I mean, yes. I'm meeting someone, er, he's over there.'

I wish that I'd arrived first, after all, so I could have watched him as he's watching me now. My feet feel clumsy and I don't know what to do with my hands as I walk to the table. My mind is full of doubt. What will he say? Will he be angry? Will he make a scene?

He stands up as I reach the table.

'Hello, Ella.' His voice is shaking.

'Hello, Dad.' My voice shakes, too. I suddenly want to burst into tears, but know I must remain cool.

He stays as still as stone, not stepping forward to hug me as he used to. I'm relieved in a way. It's too awkward, especially after all the things that were said, by both of us.

I slide onto the bench seat opposite him and we stare in silence at our menus. I'm not the least bit hungry, but when the waiter comes to take our order I ask for the crispy duck and pancakes. Dad makes a choking sound in his throat. It used to be Mum's favourite. I'm not sure if that is why I've chosen it. To get at him? I don't think so. Having pancakes to fill and roll will give me something to do when the conversation dries up. What conversation? There hasn't been any yet.

'You've no idea … ' Dad's words spit out as if they taste vile. A grey-suited lady on the next table turns round then looks away again.

I'm terrified Dad is going to lay into me in front of all these people. If he does, I'll be out of the restaurant in seconds.

'I've been going out of my mind with worry.' His voice is much quieter. 'I know you left the note saying you wouldn't be far away and that you could look after yourself, but that was no comfort. You've absolutely no idea what your disappearance has done to me.'

I swallow the lump in my throat. He's playing the emotional blackmail game; trying to make me feel guilty. Well, I'm not going to let him win.

'What do you think I've been going through?' I try to whisper, but Grey Suit is straining her ears to lap up every word. 'Do you think it was easy for *me*? I had no choice. *She* made sure of that, making my life hell before I left, and you know it.'

'But … '

The waiter appears beside him. He places a hotplate in the middle of the table. Dad seems to be holding his breath.

Determined to keep my hands steady, I unfold my serviette and put it over my lap until our plates arrive and steaming dishes of food are put on the hotplate.

'Will there be anything else, sir?'

'Water, please,' I say.

We wait in silence until two glasses of water appear in front of us. At last, in almost a whisper, Dad asks, 'So what made you suddenly decide to ring me?'

I had intended to be assertive, to demand money, to blame him for everything, but I can't speak. I stare at the shredded duck and shrug my shoulders.

'Well?' He's losing his patience with me, something he would never have done before. 'Ella, I haven't got long. We're very busy at the bank. I hope this isn't going to be a waste of my time.'

That hurts, deep inside. 'I'm your daughter,' I whisper, fighting to keep control. 'You never used to call me a waste of your time.'

He sighs and reaches for me across the table, but I snatch my hands well out of his way. He points at my food.

'Eat,' he says.

I take a pancake, fill it with duck, strips of cucumber, spring onion and plum sauce, and roll it up. But a vision of Mum flashes across my eyes and I can't bring myself to bite into it.

'I'm a bit short of money,' I mutter.

I can't tell him about the dress. It would have to be something more down to earth, like my rent or food. That wouldn't be a downright lie as I'm surviving on supermarkets' late night offers, the cheapest food I can find.

'My job pays me a pittance. I'm finding it hard to exist.'

He glances at me out of the corner of his eyes like he used to when I was small. I almost burst into tears.

'What kind of work are you doing?'

'I'm a cleaner in an office block. It was the only job I could find.'

'Ella! If you'd stayed at school … '

'Dad!'

Another silence. He picks at his food, his face expressionless. Eventually, he puts down his fork and looks straight at me.

Suddenly, in spite of everything, I need to confide in him. Ten minutes later I've told him all about how I'm living. He pulls a face at my description of Tilly and Bea, and chuckles at Velcro's name. I slowly relax as I talk and gradually he becomes more like his old self. Suddenly very hungry, I wolf down my pancake and roll another one. I realise how lovely it is to be sitting opposite him for the first time in weeks. I've missed him so much.

'I can't spare much money,' he says.

My moment of happiness vanishes. I know why he, a bank manager in charge of all that money and earning a large salary, 'can't spare much'. She has control of the purse strings. I witnessed that well before I left home.

'Would fifty pounds be enough? I think I can manage that.'

'Oh yes, thanks, Dad.'

Looking at his watch, he gasps.

'Oh no,' he says. 'The time has gone too quickly.' He shovels a few mouthfuls of his lunch into his mouth, then waves the waiter over and asks for the bill.

'I'm sorry, Ella, I have to go. I've got meetings all afternoon.'

He pays the bill. Our chat has come to an end.

'Keep in touch,' he says, but his mind is miles away by now.

I leave the restaurant five minutes later with five crumpled ten pound notes in my pocket, feeling thoroughly depressed.

Friday 19th November
Madebury

Dear Cecily

I wish you wouldn't worry so. I'm quite capable of looking after myself, though thank you for your concern.

Ella has told me a lot about herself. I knew that would explain everything. I'm not going to divulge it to you, though. That would be betraying her confidence, but I will just say how sad I am that her short life, which began so happily, has deteriorated so far.

I've begun to carry out my plan. I sent her to fetch my

cardigan from the lounge, though I only feigned feeling cold. I wanted her to see a bit more of my house. She's got a good eye, notices things, you know. Mind you, I didn't realise Jack, the untidy rascal, had left his running shoes in the middle of the lounge floor. Ella didn't say anything when she brought me my cardigan, but she's bound to have seen them. She must wonder who they belong to. I shan't tell her, of course. Not yet.

She's done the washing up each time she's been now, and a few other little things. Next time she comes, I've got a proposition to put to her. I have a feeling she might accept. I hope she'll come soon. I'm growing quite fond of her.

I'll keep you updated on how I get on.

There's one more thing. I think I've succeeded in making something else happen to her since I first met her. At times, she looks rather love-sick.

Your loving sister
Martha

15

Hazel is in an unusually good mood when I arrive at work that evening. She's humming as she polishes the glass doors in the entrance hall and she doesn't give me her normal scowl. Putting aside the vision of the overweight flamingo and keeping a very straight face, I pluck up courage and come straight out with my question.

'Overtime?' she splutters mid-tune. She stops polishing and turns to me. 'You're asking me for extra hours?'

'Yes, please,' I say. 'I need the money.'

She stares at me for a moment as if I'm crazy. She shakes her head. 'No chance.'

Realising my luck might run out any minute, I decide to risk a second question. Immediately, I see my mistake. Her mood changes in an instant. Her feathers have been ruffled.

'More money?' she squawks. 'You've got a bloody cheek. Think yourself lucky I pay you a few pence above the minimum wage. But if it's not good enough for you … '

'No, no!' I put up my hands. 'Forget I asked.' I scurry across the lobby, hoping she won't use my request as an excuse to get rid of me.

I'd looked in the newsagent's window again on my way to work, but there was nothing new. So where will I get enough money for that dress? I haven't actually found out how much it is, but I know it must be megabucks. And apart from a few pounds I've managed to save from my wages last week, I now have seventy pounds hidden in the bottom of my wardrobe.

Big deal!

As I scrub toilets, clean washbasins and mop floors, I rack my brain for any ideas of how I can earn more money. But I've been over this time and time again already. It's hopeless.

One thing keeps me going through the boredom and stink of those toilets. It's Friday. Maybe Finn will be in the Bella Casa. I might get to see him again.

The evening is clear and still at ten o'clock as I leave work with my week's wages safely in my pocket. I'm in luck. I only have to wait a few minutes before Finn leaves the café with his mates, his beautiful golden hair glowing in the lights. Watching from the same place as last time, I'm shocked when he ambles over the road right towards me. It's quite dark where I've hidden and he doesn't notice me until he's almost knocked me flying.

'Sorry.' We both speak at the same time.

Finn grips my arm to save me from landing in the gutter.

'Put her down!' shouts one of his mates.

Finn glances over his shoulder at his mates and laughs, then lets me go and sprints off towards his home.

I don't follow him. I don't need to. I know his name, where he lives, the colour of his eyes, how old he is, when his party is, two of the people who are invited. But he knows nothing about me. He probably hasn't noticed who he bumped into. Just a small, dark nobody.

Velcro is sitting at the kitchen table with a coffee when I arrive home. He beams at me and pats the chair next to his.

'You look as if you've lost fifty pounds and found a penny,' he says. 'Do you want to talk about it?'

Does my face give me away so easily?

'Don't. tell me,' he says. 'You've just seen that rugby player, but he didn't notice you. Am I right? Or am I right?'

'Are you clairvoyant?' I can't help smiling.

'No, but I remember how you looked in the café, when you confessed you fancied him.'

I sigh.

'So what's new?' he asks.

'Oh, everything.'

Velcro puts his arm round me. I don't shrug him off, but rest my head on his shoulder. He's only trying to comfort me.

'I desperately want to go to that party,' I whisper. 'Now I know it's Finn's.'

'But … '

'I know I haven't been invited … and you needn't tell me I have nothing to wear … but … promise me you won't laugh?'

'Of course I won't laugh, Ella.'

'Well, I had a dream. I was wearing a black dress and I was dancing … with someone with golden hair. I'm sure it was Finn.'

'Oh.' He looks down at me with a strange expression that could have been sadness. 'Don't set your heart on it, Ella.'

'I'm allowed to dream, aren't I?' I gently push him away and stand up.

Maybe everything will seem better in the morning.

16

Birds are flying everywhere, large black birds with enormous fingered wings, swirling around me, settling in front of me, on my head, my shoulders, my arms. They're ravens, identical to Corvus, with beady grey eyes that stare, unblinking. Their feathers shine like jet stone, glitter like rippling water. They take off, coming together into a new shape. I blink. A dress, black and shiny, is floating just above my head.

I'm twisting and turning, trying to grasp the dress. It makes me dizzy. The dress flies higher, always out of my reach. Another new shape, blurred, coming into focus. It's Sonia's face, leering, triumphant, threatening. I scream and back away, falling into someone's arms. Someone tall, strong, golden–haired.

Now it's me swirling around. I'm flying among the ravens, my body black and shiny.

Suddenly, I'm on the ground, holding binoculars to my eyes. Mum is pointing.

'A black swan,' she says.

I concentrate on a distant bird feeding by the lake. Its long elegant neck bent over, its red beak standing out against the dull mud. Red beak becoming curved and pointed, red fingernails, talons. The person next to me has changed. Mum has faded away. Sonia appears in her place.

'Now, you'll do exactly as I say,' she spits. 'Get out of this house and never come back.'

A man stands meekly behind her.

Dad, say something.

He is silent, cowed, his eyes looking downward, not meeting mine. I'm crying, pleading, but she presses her talons into his arm as he walks away.

17

It's pitch dark when I wake up, sweating. I roll over and my shaking hand feels for the bedside light. Its glow reassures me a little. I breathe deeply, but I still have such strong images flashing inside my head. That woman! She is the reason for my nightmares. Why didn't she help me get over Mum instead of tormenting me, forcing me away?

I look at the clock. Almost seven. It's so cold in my room my breath makes a fine white mist in front of my face, but I know I won't get back to sleep. Not after that nightmare.

Ten minutes later, I let myself out of the front door and jog along the road. Not caring where I go, I want to run the hideous images out of my brain.

I pass Luigi's, all in darkness, and jog along the High Street, still lit by street lamps and the headlights of cars. It's just beginning to get light as I cross over by the Bella Casa and climb the hill. Breathing heavily, I easily remember the route to his house. I stop outside the driveway and bend double, hands on knees, gasping for breath.

Is Finn awake yet? I picture him stretching as he climbs out of bed. His hair is tousled and his deep brown eyes dazed with sleep. Has he been dreaming of me?

I snap myself out of these mad thoughts. Of course he hasn't. I reluctantly drag myself away, turning and running back the way I've come.

The sun is coming up as I reach Martha's road. As before, I haven't realised I'm heading that way. Something draws me there. I feel better for the run, but now I'm close to Corvus, the raven part of the dream comes back. What does it all mean?

I'm miles away in my thoughts. Suddenly, out of nowhere, another jogger shoots past me and speeds along Martha's road. I stop and lean on a wall, panting, and watch him. He's wearing a black sweatband on his cropped dark head and a green vest and shorts. His trainers are black with white stripes down the sides. I turn away. It's time I went back to the house. I need a shower.

I take one last look along Martha's road before turning back into the High Street. The jogger was there only a few seconds ago, but now he has gone.

18

No sooner has my hand left the knocker a few hours later than the door creaks open, as if Martha has been waiting on the other side of the door. Her welcoming smile tells me she's pleased to see me. I'm glad to see her, too. I take my coat off in the hall, hang it on a hook on the old hat-stand and turn to face Corvus.

I blink, startled. I'm sure he winked. What's going on? I gawp at him, but he only stares back at me. I must have imagined it. Pushing thoughts of a winking raven away, I follow Martha along the corridor.

'Tea?'

We've established a routine. I'm already putting the kettle on and she's seated herself in her usual chair with her handbag on the table, next to an empty cup and saucer. But then she stands up.

'Will you excuse me?' she asks, as she makes for a door at the side of the kitchen. 'I just need to fetch something.'

She totters from the room and closes the door. I hum as I pile the washing up in the sink and wait for the kettle to boil, thanking my lucky stars that she came into my life. I go to the table to fetch the cup and saucer. I am just about to move Martha's handbag so I can wipe the table, when I see it is open. I gasp and step back, almost tripping over my own feet. There's a fat wad of twenty-pound notes sticking out of the top of the bag. Wow! What I could buy with all that!

I feel ashamed, remembering how tempted I had been by her ring. Nothing would make me steal a penny from Martha now. With shaking hands, I carry the cup and saucer to the sink. After a few minutes, the door opens and Martha comes back in. She sits down in her chair.

'Ella, would you fetch me my slippers from the lounge, please? My feet get very cold these days.'

'OK.'

Corvus and I eye each other in the hall.

'Did you wink at me earlier?' I ask.

He doesn't move a muscle. I shake my head. I definitely imagined it!

'Silly me,' I chuckle. 'You're only an old stuffed bird.'

Was that muffled caw coming from his beak? It can't have been. I'm even more off my head than I thought.

I fetch Martha's slippers, noticing that the trainers are no longer in the lounge, then hurry back to the kitchen.

'I want to talk to you,' says Martha as I help her put the slippers on. 'Sit down.'

Why does my heart race as I do as she asked? What is she going to say?

'I've been thinking,' she begins, as soon as I'm facing her across the table. 'As you know I've been concerned about you.'

'Me, too … about you, I mean.'

Where is this leading?

'You've told me enough about yourself for me to know that your life is troubled. One day perhaps you'll feel like telling me more, but I don't want to pry if you don't want to … '

'I … '

'Now is not the time,' she says with a smile. 'Now is for being positive.'

Her smile is infectious and I smile back, though I still have no clue what she is getting at.

'I have a proposition for you.'

'Yes?' My voice comes out as a squeak.

'I guess you are in need of money. Is there something you wish to buy?'

I lower my eyes, embarrassed. How does she know so much about me? And what is her proposition?

'You've been so helpful to me … I knew you would from the moment our paths crossed. And I know I can trust you … '

I open my mouth to speak, but she puts up her hand.

'You could have taken advantage of me … my ring … the temptation must have been enormous. You told me yourself that I should be careful someone didn't steal it. That person could have been you.'

I nod. No point in denying I hadn't thought of it.

'And the money I left here on the table just now ... you didn't touch it ... '

The kettle is boiling madly, filling the corner of the kitchen with clouds of steam. Heat rising to my face, I leap from the table and rush to turn it off. She'd left the money there to tempt me and then sent me out of the room afterwards so she could count it. Should I feel annoyed? I tell myself I ought not to be. She's only making sure I'm trustworthy. Making the tea helps calm me down. A few moments later, I bring two cups to the table. Martha nods at my chair and I sit down.

'I hope you aren't offended by my little tests,' she says. 'I just wanted to make sure before ... well ... it's like this ... I'd like to see you more often.'

My surprise must have shown on my face.

'I'd like you to visit me ... for a cup of tea and a chat ... I enjoy your company, but ... would you think it beneath you to do my housework, too? I'd pay you well. I can't manage to do it myself any more, as I'm sure you've noticed. I'm too old and I've grown fond of you. I'd love someone I trust to help me.'

I'm even more amazed. I can understand her reasons for testing me, but she just said she's fond of me! Am I fond of her? I can't explain why, but I guess I am, even though I've known her for such a short time. I take a sip of tea. Its warmth is comforting. I haven't felt this content since before Mum died.

'Thank you,' I whisper. 'I'd love to work for you, Martha.'

I want to rush round the table and hug her, but I hold back. I don't know how she'd react and I don't want to ruin everything.

She potters into the hall and opens the cupboard under the stairs, showing me the vacuum cleaner and other stuff I will need. Corvus glares at me, but I don't let him bother me as I carry the cleaner to the lounge.

Two hours later, Martha hands me some money. 'This is for the work you've already done out of the kindness of your heart. And for today's chores.'

'Thanks.'

'Will you come tomorrow?'

I nod and smile.

When I leave her house, I hurry to Luigi's to celebrate my good luck. Luigi raises his eyebrows when I order my cappuccino.

'But it's not Friday, Missi,' he says. 'And you're looking very happy today.'

I grin. I guess he's only seen me looking miserable before. I go to sit at the table by the window where I first saw Martha.

I pat my pocket where two crisp purple twenty-pound notes are hidden. At this rate, I'll have enough money for the dress in no time.

19

The dress is still in the shop window. I stare at it for several minutes before daring to go inside. I find it on a rack at the rear of the shop. I wonder if they have my size. Luckily, they have. I pull out a size eight.

'Would you like to try that on?' The shop assistant is wearing a label that says 'Beverley'. She smiles. 'I love that dress, don't you? It's very reasonably priced.'

I still have no idea how much. I've purposely avoided finding out. I want to be sure it looks as good on me as it does on the mannequin in the window before worrying about that.

It does! I've brought a hair clasp with me so I can put my hair up. When I've slipped into the dress and done up the zip, I turn to look at myself in the mirror. I gasp. Even without make-up, I've become a completely different person. I know this will wow Finn. I *have* to have it. And I *have* to get to his party.

'Can I come in?' Beverley pushes the curtain aside and peers around it. 'That's just perfect,' she gushes. 'It was made for you. Are you going somewhere nice?'

I mutter something about a party, wishing I could feel more confident about everything.

When she's gone, I slip the dress off and pull my jeans and sweater back on. Time to read the price tag ... I swallow hard and take some deep breaths. It's almost two hundred pounds! How long will it take me to earn that much? And I'll need shoes and a small bag, and some glittery jewellery, which means another hundred at least. The party is only two weeks away.

'So are you going to buy the dress?' Beverley asks, as I hand it back to her.

'I'll have to think about it.'

Her face blanks me out and she hurries to hang up the dress.

When I reach the house, I run up to my room and find the old shoe in my wardrobe. With the money from Martha and Dad, and the small amount I've saved from my wages, I now have £119. I sit on my bed and try to think. Maybe I'll be able to find some shoes in a charity shop. And there's a department store in the next town that has a great jewellery department. I've browsed there several times. It isn't expensive.

'I'll try there,' I mutter as I shove the shoe back in the wardrobe.

Voices jangle up the stairs. The Snob Sisters are home. They sound so excited I'm about to creep down to eavesdrop, when I realise their voices are getting closer. They come upstairs, pass my bedroom and go towards Tilly's room at the front of the house. I open my door a crack and peer out. They are both carrying large carrier bags with a boutique logo printed on the side. They've bought their dresses.

I'd been right when I said they'd both look fantastic. Red is the perfect colour for Bea, and Tilly's silver dress sets off her copper hair brilliantly. They parade up and down the landing, flaunting themselves like a pair of peacocks. I force a grin and nod and tell them how wonderful they look, but inside I'm feeling hopeless.

I go back into my room and sit on the bed, staring blankly at the wall. How can I ever hope to outshine the Snob Sisters?

I snap myself out of my mood. What's the matter with me? I don't usually give up this easily. I'm determined to win. And the only prize I want is Finn.

Downstairs, I find a road atlas and search the local page for Critchley Manor, but there is no mention of it. I listen up the stairs. The Snob Sisters are still busy preening themselves. I quickly log onto Bea's computer and google Critchley Manor. Wow! What a place to have a party! Beside the photo of the manor there is a map. Now I know where to find it, only about a mile out of town.

Returning to my room, I change into my trainers then leave the house. There will just be time for me to find the place before it gets dark and before I have to be at work.

Heading out of town in the opposite direction to Finn's house, I jog at a steady pace, keeping to the pavements at first, then hugging the side of the road as it leads out into the countryside.

After about twenty minutes, I reach a large sign outside a pair of ornate cast-iron gates. I've arrived. The gates are closed, but I peer through them, along the drive to the manor. I can't help thinking how perfect it would be if the next time I come here I'll be in Finn's arms, wearing that black dress.

Suddenly, the gates click and shudder then slowly swing open. I step back. A silver Mercedes comes up the drive, sweeps through the gates and stops at the edge of the road. The driver is a fair-haired woman wearing dark glasses. Next to her is a bald man, who glares at me as they wait for traffic to clear. Then I see who is sitting in the back of the car. Finn!

My heart flips in double somersaults. Finn does a double take, as if he remembers seeing me somewhere before. Would he remember the girl on the touch line at rugby, or the one outside the café? I raise my hand, but he turns away as the car speeds off.

I suppose they must have been in there sorting things out for the party. My body all of a quiver, I curse under my breath. Why do I have to look my worst when he's around?

As I jog back into town I have one positive thought. At least I now know where I'm going to gate-crash!

20

I hadn't realised how enormous Martha's house is. It's much too big for one little old lady. Or is there someone else there, too? The trainers still puzzle me. And who owns the car I've seen parked in the driveway? It's time I asked Martha.

Apart from the lounge, which Martha raves about and says looks really smart after my cleaning, there is a dining room and another smaller room off that, and a kind of study, all on the ground floor. I guess there must be quite a few bedrooms upstairs. No wonder Martha can't cope with the housework.

I set to work on the study as soon as I arrive the next day. It's rather early for our usual cup of tea. The dust is so thick I have to cover my mouth and nose with my scarf as I vacuum the carpet, and I have to empty the dust bag twice! But I don't mind. It's a million times better than cleaning smelly toilets under Hazel's watchful eyes, and I've finished it in an hour.

I try not to be nosy. Honestly, I do. I don't want to take advantage of Martha's kindness, but I can't help noticing several letters on the desk while I'm dusting it. They are addressed to Mrs M Wainwright. So now I know Martha's surname. But then I spot a large white envelope addressed to Mr J Bartrum. Is this the owner of the trainers and the car? It seems more and more likely that Martha does not live alone. I wonder who Mr J Bartrum is.

On the mantelpiece, there's a photo of a young man. Well, he looks a few years older than me. He's got dark hair and brown eyes. Could he be Mr J Bartrum? He looks somehow familiar.

Corvus definitely winks at me, I swear it, as I go to the hall to put the vacuum cleaner and dusters away in the cupboard under the stairs. I wink back and grin at him. If my friends could see me they'd send for men in white coats to take me away. But I've grown apart from Jodie and Claire and Anna and the others since that evil woman clawed her way into my life and made me shrivel up inside. So I haven't contacted any of them since I left home. I've blotted them out of my mind. I bet they've forgotten me already. And they can't see me now … no one can, so it doesn't matter.

I reach up and touch the raven's shiny back. My fingers ripple over the thin bone-like shafts and the smoother outer vanes of his feathers.

'Mum taught me all about feathers,' I whisper. 'She was an ornithologist.'

We're sitting in Mum's study surrounded by birds' feathers of every size, shape and colour. They are mounted and labelled ... 'Blackbird', 'Wren', 'Yellowhammer', 'Raven'. She's compiling a book about British birds.

She lays a tiny feather on a slide and pushes it under the microscope.

'Look at this,' she says. 'It's from a fledgling blue tit. It's a miracle.'

I peer down the lens at the amazing patterns of this tiny thing. Mum's right. It's so fantastic ... the feather of a young bird just learning to fly.

I feel Corvus raise his head a little higher under my hand.

'No wonder Martha's kept you all these years,' I whisper. 'You're rather a handsome chap!'

Martha has been asleep and wakes with a start when the kitchen door clicks behind me. She blinks a few times as if she's trying to remember who I am. Then she smiles, but I'm worried about her again. Is it normal for old people to nod off quite so easily in the middle of the day?

'Have you got something on your mind, dear?' she asks quietly, as we sit on our usual chairs, teacups in front of us a few minutes later. 'I have a feeling that something's happened to you since we first met. Someone you've fallen for perhaps?'

Heat spreads up my face. How can she guess about

Finn? I nod and sigh. Will she understand if I tell her about him?

'It's only a boy,' I mutter.

'Ah.' Martha's eyes light up as if she's delighted.

I have a really strange feeling that she has guessed.

'I don't really know him,' I gabble. 'I've only seen him a few times. And he's having a party … I'd really love to go.'

She nods and folds her arms. I have no idea why I am telling her all this, but I can't stop myself pouring it all out.

'My housemates are invited, but I'm not … of course I'm not. He doesn't even know me … but … Tilly and Bea, that's the other girls in the house …they've just bought dresses … and I've seen a beautiful dress, but there's no way I can afford it … '

'Ah,' Martha says again. 'I guessed you needed the money for something very special.'

That week, I clean the whole of the downstairs thoroughly and agree to do the bedrooms the following week, but I don't pluck up courage to ask her about the car or Mr J Bartum. I search for food bargains in the supermarket and try to eat less, so I save more of my office-cleaner earnings to go with what Martha gives me. By the end of the week, I have £176 in my shoe.

On my way to my Friday night treat in Luigi's, I pass by the dress shop. It's still open so I pop inside and make for the back of the shop. I need to see and touch the dress that I'll soon be able to afford. I find the rail and go through the hangers, size 14, size 10, size 12, size 10, size 12. No size eight! Feeling sick, I dash to the cash desk. There is no sign of Beverley.

'That black dress,' I pant, pointing. 'You had a size eight the other day. It's gone. Have you got another one?'

The girl shakes her head.

'What about the one in the window?'

She ambles over to the front of the shop and takes an age investigating the size of that dress while I fidget about, hopping from one foot to the other.

'Size 14,' she says, as she emerges from the window.

'Could you check that the size eight isn't behind the counter, or in the changing rooms?'

She looks at me with a bored expression in her eyes.

'We sold the size eight yesterday.'

I gasp. 'Could you order another one for me, please? I need it for Saturday.'

'Nah, sorry. That's the end of the range.'

I turn away, devastated, leaving the shop before I make a fool of myself.

21

I rush back to the house and barge into the kitchen. 'It's gone!'

Velcro is sitting at the table, his head bent over a book. He swivels round and his pale eyes look up at me.

'What's gone?'

'The dress, that fantastic dress I saw in the shop.' I burst into tears. 'How can I go to the party now?'

Velcro pulls out a chair. I flop down next to him, weak-kneed. Like last time, his arm creeps round me. Like last time, I sink my head onto his shoulder and he waits for me to calm down.

'Ella,' he says softly. 'You have to be realistic. It was all wishful thinking. A dream inside your head.'

I pull away, wiping my eyes on my sleeve.

'No! I really want to go. And I've *got* to have that dress.'

He frowns. He must think I'm off my head. I'm beginning to believe so, too. I've never been so irrational or demanding before.

'There are other dresses,' Velcro says.

Other dresses? When I've set my heart on that one? I don't answer. It's safer that way. I don't want to say anything rude to hurt his feelings.

In silence, I make myself a coffee.

'Aren't you going to Luigi's this evening?' he asks.

I shake my head. 'I don't feel like it now.'

I wander up to my room and lie on my bed. I have to sort out my brain. Of course, Velcro is right. It *is* a dream. But it's become so important to me. I don't want it to be dashed. I've worked hard, almost saved enough money. It isn't fair.

After work that night, I wander around in the cold darkness. I don't want to go back to the house. The Snob Sisters are bound to be babbling on about everything to do with the party. I couldn't stand that, especially if they order me to help them or ask my opinion on anything. I might say something that's not repeatable. And it might make me lose my cheap accommodation.

In Martha's street, the wind lifts leaves from the pavements and swirls them up and around my head like a flock of starlings. I duck, then put my hands in my pockets and shuffle along, not stopping until I reach Martha's gates. The car is there. I glance up at the round tower. Curtains are closed, but there's a light in the window.

I hurry home and slide into bed, wondering how life has become so complicated.

Dancers fill the room in a mass of bodies. A red dress, a silver one mixed in with the rest, a rainbow of colours. And the black dress. Someone is wearing it. But that someone is not me. Fighting to keep on my feet as the crowd sways and surges, I feel a cold draught down my back. I glance down in horror. I'm naked.

Laughter echoes all around me. Fingers point. I cover myself with my hands and arms and dash for the door. It's locked. The laughter turns to a shriek then a loud caw, as a large black bird flies in at the window.

At first, I think it's a raven, but slowly I recognise its shape. Its shoulders hunched, long neck hooked, beak vicious, talons red. The laughter is piercing, the head is thrown back. My step-mother faces me, hands on hips.

'Get out and never come back,' she shrieks.

I'm still having flashbacks from this latest dream as I head back to Martha's on Monday morning, after a miserable weekend. I mutter to myself all the way. I haven't got over losing the dress.

I'm startled when the door opens before I can even knock. Martha doesn't seem to notice my gloomy expression, but beckons me inside, a mischievous smile on her face, as if she knows something I don't. I look up at Corvus, but he stares straight ahead. He isn't giving anything away.

'Will you clean a couple of bedrooms today, dear?' The twinkle is still in Martha's eyes. 'The ones to the left when you get to the top of the stairs?'

'OK.' I try to smile back.

'Don't go in any of the others rooms, please. Nor up the second flight of stairs at the far end of the landing.'

'OK,' I repeat. Those stairs must lead up into the tower. And I guess it's Mr J's room. I wonder if he's her lodger. I'm dying to ask her who he is, but I don't want her to think I'm too nosy, so I resist the temptation again.

I wait for Martha to explain why she is looking so excited, but she goes to her chair and sits down with her back to me. I hear a strange sound as if she's chuckling. Puzzled, I fetch the cleaning equipment. Corvus sits guarding the stairs. I wonder if he'll let me pass.

There's a glint in his eyes, but he doesn't show any kind of recognition as I step onto the first tread and climb the stairs. I stand at the top and look along the landing. There are two doors on the left and four more on the right. At the far end of the landing, there is an archway and I can just make out the narrow flight of stairs going up. My feet itch to explore up there, but my conscience forbids it. I begin to concentrate on my job. No point in jeopardising that.

The bedrooms, like the rest of the house, could be part of a museum: faded curtains and bedcovers, and furniture that was probably bought fifty years ago. There are porcelain vases and bowls and jugs, all of them beautifully decorated with exotic birds. They look quite valuable. I'm careful not to drop them as I dust them. When I've cleaned both rooms, I'm gasping for a cup of tea so I hurry downstairs.

'All done,' I whisper to Corvus and, ever so slightly, his head nods.

Martha appears to be asleep as usual, but as soon as I reach the kitchen she bounces out of her chair so fast I'm scared for her safety. The grin is still on her face.

'Sit down.' It comes out sharply like an order.

'But … ' I'm going to say I haven't made the tea yet, but her expression stops me. I sit down at the table.

'Close your eyes.'

I do as I'm told, listening to her shuffling footsteps, the creak of a cupboard door and the rustling of paper.

What's she up to?

Something is put in front of me.

'Open.' It's a flat parcel, wrapped in gold paper with a silver ribbon tied neatly round it.

'For me?'

She nods, her hands clasped together and her feet almost dancing on the tiles. She's like a little girl at Christmas.

My fingers are clumsy and I take a while to undo the ribbon and peel off the paper. I stare and grip the table to steady my dizzy head. How could she have known? It's black. The sequins glitter in a ray of sunlight through the window pane. It's size eight.

It's the dress!

Monday 6th December
Madebury

My dear Cecily

You may wonder at my silence over the past couple of weeks, but rest assured, I've been too busy to write and you'll be delighted to hear that my plan continues to go perfectly. Ella is as good a worker as I hoped she would be and I've paid her well for it.

I now know how strong my power is over her.

In my attempt to bring the poor girl some happiness, I appear to have made her fall head over heels for the first boy who crossed her path. He's a good-looking rich teenager who happens to be acquainted with Ella's housemates. She seems truly smitten.

This is not exactly what I had planned. I will have to take any action necessary when the time comes.

My cleverness doesn't end there. Following her mentioning a dress she had her eye on for a party she would love to go to, I did something even you would be impressed with. Ella almost fainted when she opened a parcel I gave her and found the very dress she desired.

I haven't felt so light-hearted for years. I feel truly rejuvenated! A mere girl of eighty-five! And, you'll be glad to hear, I still have several tricks up my sleeve, but no more of that for now. Suffice to say, Corvus and I are keeping a measured eye on her.

She doesn't know about Jack, though if she has any powers of deduction she will have guessed that someone lives here with me. Apart from the running shoes she must have seen in the lounge (did I tell you about those?), she will have noticed his car outside when she has passed by in the evenings (Corvus has spotted her on several occasions) and I purposely left a letter addressed to Jack on my desk in the study and a photograph of him on the mantelpiece.

I have forbidden her to mount the stairs into the tower so that will make her all the more curious. I want to keep it that way.

I promise I will keep you informed of developments.

Your loving sister

Martha

22

I can't help wondering if Martha is a witch. I don't mean in a bad witch sense, like the Wicked Witch of the West in *The Wizard of Oz*. More like the good witch, keeping watch over me. And Corvus has some kind of magic power, too. He winks at me so hard on my way out I'm afraid he'll fall off his newel post. Either way, I feel bewitched!

Since I unwrapped that parcel and hugged Martha so strongly I was in danger of crushing her delicate bones, I haven't stopped shaking. I head straight for Luigi's. It's the best place to chill out and get over the shock. Stirring my cappuccino and watching it swirl calms me so I can think more clearly. The party is on Saturday, only five days away. I now have the dress and quite a bit of money, enough to buy some shoes and jewellery. The best place is Bishop's, the department store in

Fernton. I've got time to go there and back on the bus before work.

After a twenty-minute bus ride, I find the store and hurry inside. I've been in this store so often, but always to browse, never to buy. The jewellery is on the edge of the ladies' dress department on the ground floor. I begin to finger the necklaces, bracelets and earrings. A glittering necklace catches my eye. I unhook it from the stand and do up the clasp at the back of my neck. I peer at myself in the mirror and sigh. It isn't real diamonds, of course, but who could tell? It's beautiful. It would go perfectly with the black dress.

I'm concentrating on the jewellery, so I don't take much notice of the woman at first. It's like any woman talking to a young shop assistant. Their conversation mingles with other sounds in the department store.

Then the woman laughs, high-pitched and brittle, like shattering glass. I shudder. That laugh reminds me of someone I've been trying unsuccessfully to wipe from my mind. I glance across the store. I see a tall slim woman, dressed in a short black pencil skirt and fitted jacket, and black thigh boots with very high heels. She has her back to me. The shop assistant is smiling up at her, raising her eyebrows as if hoping her customer likes the long red dress she is showing her.

Feeling suddenly cold, I clutch my coat around me and step behind a rack of dresses. I want to observe this woman in secret. The woman tosses her head, making her blonde hair shimmer in the shop lights. Her hand reaches up to pat the perfectly neat bob. She has long elegant fingers, the manicured nails a slash of blood red, like talons after the kill.

'Oh, yes, Amy,' she says in a voice as sugary as candyfloss. 'In this dress, I'd be sure to turn a few heads. I'd be the belle of the ball!' She tosses her head again. 'I'll try it on in a moment. What else have you got?'

'I'll go and see, madam.' Amy hurries away.

I try to push down the nausea that is rising in my throat.

The woman turns. I duck down, my heart pounding. Crouching low, I peer through the clothing on the rack. I gasp. The sharp nose and chin; the heavy black eye make-up and thin arched line of the eyebrows; the piercing blue eyes and blood-red lips. That could only mean one person. Sonia!

Sonia tosses her head as her eyes scour the store. She paces up and down, sighing, glaring at her watch. I bury myself deeper into the clothing, terrified that Sonia will come in my direction. I dare not let her see me. I clench my fists, digging my nails into the palms of my hands to drive away the nausea and stop the sensation that I'm going to faint.

'Ah. At last.' There is a cutting edge to Sonia's voice. She has been kept waiting, not something she is willing to tolerate, I remember.

I dare to peep. Sonia has turned away again and is looming over Amy, who has returned with two new dresses.

'No! This one is dreadful.' The edge is sharpening. Sonia thrusts a blue dress aside. 'And so is this one.' She waves the second one away with a toss of her head. 'Haven't you got anything better?'

'This seems to be all we've got in your size, madam.'

I detect a tremble in Amy's voice. 'Would you like to try the red one?'

'I'm not sure that I can be bothered now.'

I shudder. Sonia's voice is harsh, rasping like a saw. 'It really is a disgrace. You've kept me waiting and can only offer me one miserable dress. You're useless.'

'B – but, madam. That's all we have at present.'

'This store is a scandal.'

There is silence for a moment.

'But … you did like the red one, madam.' I cringe at the grovelling tone of Amy's voice, but I know Sonia will lap it up. 'And you were right. If you wear this dress everyone will turn to look at you.'

'Mmm.'

'You said yourself that you'll be the belle of the ball.'

I can imagine a gleam in Sonia's eyes as she tosses her head again.

Suddenly, I have a desperate need to get out of there. I can't stand being in the same building as that dreadful woman. I dodge between racks of clothing and half-run for the door.

As I step out onto the pavement, I feel a heavy weight thump onto my shoulder. My stomach churns as I glance sideways and see the wrinkled skin and thick black hairs on the back of a hand. I swivel my head and look up into the dark eyes of a man in uniform. His face is like a mask, without expression.

'We've been watching you!'

My mind freezes. I can't understand what he means.

'You've been acting suspiciously,' says the man. 'You'd better come with me.'

I wish he didn't have to be speaking so loudly. I'm aware of eyes turning in our direction.

'I – I was just browsing,' I stutter. 'I wasn't doing anything wrong.'

'Inside, *now*.' The man spits out the order. He lifts his hand from my shoulder and grips my arm firmly.

My legs are shaking and I feel very wobbly as I step back inside the store.

'The manager wants to speak to you.'

'But why? What have I done?'

At that moment, I smell a heady scent of perfume. *Raptor*! I recognise it instantly. Sonia's favourite!

'Hello, my sweet! How wonderful to see you!' The sugary tones are back.

A chill creeps up my spine as I turn slowly to face my step-mother, the last person on earth I need at that moment. I glance up at the cold blue eyes that hold just a suspicion of amusement.

I don't speak. Why should I greet a woman I hate so much?

Sonia turns to the security man and flutters her false eyelashes at him.

'Now what's all this about, honey?' Sickly sugar drools from her lips.

'Do you know this girl?' The man's face remains expressionless.

'Of course I know her, honey. She's my lovely step-daughter.' She smiles.

I've seen that smile before: just before the kill.

'Won't you just tell me what she's supposed to have done?' Sonia is feigning the cute creature she is not.

The security man blinks. He doesn't answer the question, but tightens his grip on my arm. I know I should complain. What right has he to touch me? But I'm totally intimidated by Sonia.

'Undo your coat,' the man hisses in my ear. 'Show your step-mother that necklace you are concealing.'

I gasp and my hand flies to my throat. The beautiful glittering necklace is still there. I'd completely forgotten it as soon as I recognised Sonia.

'I … I wasn't going to steal it,' I cry. I look at Sonia for help. Perhaps she will forget what's happened between us in the past and speak up for me.

But Sonia's lips are twisting into a contorted grin and her eyes, so cold a moment ago, flash with fire.

'Of course you were!' she rasps, a lethal talon pointing straight at me. 'Quite the young thief, this one. She deserves everything you can throw at her.'

My mouth gapes open. I don't believe it. This evil, vile woman has gone further than even I would have expected.

'No!' I yell as I escape the man's grip and lunge at my step-mother.

Sonia steps lightly aside. She cackles. Then, in a split second, she switches her demeanour again and, with a toss of the head, she walks away.

23

'Come on,' says the security man, his mask remaining unmoved.

I fight back the tears, feeling stunned. Moving like a zombie, I follow him between racks of clothes, past several gawking customers to the other side of the shop. He stops by a door and punches a code into a keypad. The door swings open onto a flight of stairs.

'Up.'

As I climb the stairs, all the pent-up anger and hatred begin to rise in my throat. I grasp the banister rail hard to stop myself hitting out. Tears of frustration flow down my cheeks. I've got enough misery in my life. I don't need any more. We reach a landing and the security man raps sharply on a door. I blow my nose and grit my teeth. I'm not going to let them accuse me of something I haven't done!

'Yes?' A woman's voice calls from inside.

'In you go.' He turns the handle and pushes the door. We step into a very small room, lit by one tiny window high up in the ceiling. The door closes. Seated behind a desk, the woman looks severe with her short dark hair and black-rimmed glasses. Trapped between the woman and the man right behind me, my chest tightens and I find it hard to breathe. I lean forward and grip the desk.

'Another shop-lifter?' She glares at me over her glasses.

'No, you've got it wrong,' I gasp.

The man points at my neck.

'She took this necklace outside the shop. What more evidence do you want?'

'But ... '

He interrupts me, before I can protest. 'Her step-mother was there to witness it. Says this young lady is a thief.'

'You don't want to take any notice of her,' I shout. 'She hates me ... she'd say anything ... '

The woman holds up her hand. 'Let's take this calmly.' She frowns. 'So, Bert, where is this witness?'

'One minute she was there, then the next ... '

'You should have asked her to come with you ... '

'No!' My voice wobbles. 'She's evil ... '

'Well, let me see. I should call the police ... '

'No! Please ... '

' ... or perhaps I should listen to your side of the story.'

I take a deep breath and almost collapse onto the chair she indicates.

'Thank you, Bert. Go downstairs and see if you can find the step-mother.'

I open my mouth to protest, but the woman glares at me. Bert grunts and leaves the room. She switches on a lamp. The sky is darkening above us.

'I ... it was a mistake,' I say. I undo the clasp and drop the necklace onto her desk.

'So you say.' She peers at it then frowns up at me. 'Let's start at the beginning. What's your name?'

For a second, I think about giving a false name, but decide against it. 'Ella Sharma.'

'Age?'

'Sixteen.'

'And your parents, apart from your step-mother?'

'Mum's dead.' I bite my lip and pause until the need to cry wears off. 'Dad's a bank manager.'

She gives me a long hard look, as if sussing out my life. 'Right, the best thing we can do is call him ... '

'No!' I cover my face in my hands. I can't bear the thought of Dad seeing me in trouble.

'I'm sorry, but you have no choice. You're underage, so you need a parent or guardian with you, even if we don't involve the police.'

'OK.' Reluctantly, I give her Dad's number. She dials and speaks to him. I hear his raised voice as she talks.

'He's on his way,' she says when she's rung off.

There is a knock at the door. Bert puts his head round it.

'No sign of her,' he grunts.

The woman sighs and nods, and Bert's head retreats. I feel some of the tension draining from me.

The wait for Dad to arrive seems like hours. I have to sit in silence while the woman reads papers and signs a few letters. I try to breathe deeply, to stay cool, and think about Finn, the party, Martha and Corvus and the dress. I think about Mum, the good times before she became ill.

At last, there is another knock. All my determination to stay cool disappears as soon as Dad opens the door and comes into the room. I fling myself into his arms and sob. After a while, he gently pushes me away and holds me at arm's length, bending to look into my eyes. He's frowning and he has dark rings round his eyes. Then he turns to the woman.

'I'm Ella's dad, Adler Sharma.'

'Jane Whiting.'

They shake hands.

'What's this all about, Ms Whiting?'

'I'm afraid your daughter was caught leaving the store wearing this necklace.' She points. 'She had not paid for it.'

'Ella, is this true?'

I can tell Dad hasn't spoken to Sonia. That's a great relief. He only knows what Ms Whiting has told him. I'd hate him to think I meant to steal the necklace, but he won't have forgotten I asked him for money such a short while ago. I decide to tell the truth and hope they will believe me. Surely Dad will be able to judge if I'm lying or not. He always could before Sonia took him over.

'I didn't mean to,' I begin. 'I mean … well … Sonia suddenly appeared and … well … I panicked.'

Half an hour later, Dad and I leave Ms Whiting's room. It seems they believed me. I've been let off with what Ms Whiting said was 'a caution'. Dad paid for the necklace, though I don't want it after all that trouble. But I didn't refuse it. It's the first thing he's bought me for a while.

It's dark outside and the shop is about to close. My legs don't want to support my body and I cling to Dad's arm as he leads me to his car. He used to be so springy, but he's plodding now as if he's carrying a great weight. And I don't mean me.

'I'll take you home.'

As we climb into the car, I look at my watch and gasp. It's 5.40.

'Oh no. I'm going to be late for work. I'll get the sack.'

He starts the engine. 'Where to?'

'Madebury.'

As he stops outside the office block fifteen minutes later he leans over and kisses my cheek. 'Bye, Ella. Keep in touch.'

'OK.' I think he means it. He's feeling so miserable, I can tell. Is he regretting marrying Sonia? I really, really hope so!

I wish he'd suggested meeting up again, but at least I now know he'll come when I need him. And I won't forget that he kissed me.

24

It's well past midnight. I can't sleep. My brain's in overdrive.

Why? Apart from dealing with my traumatic experience in Bishop's this afternoon and thinking about Finn, I suddenly twigged something while I was mopping out the toilets at work this evening.

Doh! Why didn't I get it before? It all adds up. The trainers, the envelope, the photo in Martha's study. I knew I'd seen him somewhere before. He's the jogger. Not a bad looker, but not in the gorgeous sense like Finn.

But why hasn't Martha told me about Mr J Bartrum? She must realise I've guessed there's someone else living there with her, but why the secrecy? I wonder what his first name is.

I haven't seen Finn lately. He hasn't been in the Bella Casa when I've peered in, and apart from jogging past his house I'm not sure where else I'll find him. According to the Snob Sisters, he's in his final year at school, but I can't ask them which one. They'd get suspicious. I'll just have to wait – and dream. If I close my eyes, I can imagine he's near me. Asleep or awake, I can hear his voice, see his face.

It'll soon be Tuesday morning, his party only four days away. Then my dreams will come true. I'm totally in love with the dress. What a fantastic person Martha is! How can I ever thank her enough? Now I just have to buy shoes, a handbag and jewellery. No money worries, thanks to her.

I haven't told Velcro about the dress. He's been a great listener and a shoulder to cry on, but I don't tell him everything. I've got to have a few private thoughts and secrets. And anyway, I've got Martha to confide in now. Maybe I'll tell Velcro on the day of the party, surprise him. That way I can be sure he won't snitch on me to the others. Not that I think he would.

I'm wearing the dress, dancing, swirling in someone's arms. It's the same dream at first, but suddenly, the dress shreds into a million feathers, blown away by a fierce wind. I'm screaming, running into blackness. Then Corvus is there, his slate-grey eyes out-staring mine. His black claws change colour. Red. Always red. The colour of her talon-varnish.

I must have slept eventually. I've woken late with that horrible vision of *her* in my mind. I shove it away.

Shoes. I've got to look my best at the party. The dress will look even better with the right shoes.

I'm nervous about going into shops in case I do something stupid again. You won't catch me going anywhere near that department store. I don't think they'd welcome me there and I might run the risk of bumping into *her*.

I stay in Madebury. Now I don't need the money for the dress, I can afford decent shoes, but I'm not going to go mad. So I avoid the shops where you need a mortgage to buy. I wish some of my old friends could be with me. We'd have had a real laugh and made nuisances of ourselves, trying on every pair of shoes in every shop. But I'm on my own. It's not the same.

In the second shop I go into, I find a pair of shiny black shoes with pointy toes and stiletto heels. Reasonable price. I ask for my size and try them on, walk around the shop in them without breaking my ankle. Perfect! A tiny black handbag on a thin silver chain matches the shoes. I'm almost sorted. I pay for them and leave the shop without being arrested. And I've got plenty of money left for jewellery.

The necklace that Dad paid for is hidden away with the money. I suppose I could wear it if I'm desperate, but I've got a few days to search for a better one, plus earrings. Maybe I'll find something tomorrow. If I'm going to sweep my hair up on top of my head for the party I'll need a clasp, too. Something shiny to contrast with my black hair.

Martha is still wearing the mischievous smile when she opens the door to me. I show her the shoes and bag, and thank her again for the dress. Her mood rubs off on me and excitement bubbles up inside. But then I have a flashback of meeting Sonia in Fernton and my heart freezes in my chest. I don't want to breathe a word about my little mistake to Martha. It might destroy her trust in me.

'What's troubling you, dear?'

I gasp. My thoughts must have shown on my face. 'Oh … it's nothing really … something that happened yesterday.'

She puts her head on one side like an inquisitive bird, but she doesn't expect me to say any more. That's what I like about her. She's probably dying to know the truth, but she always waits for me to tell her … only if I want to. I realise I do want to … at least, part of it.

'I met my step-mother.' I shudder.

'How terrible for you.' Her voice is quiet and so full of sympathy I'm tempted to tell all, but I feel too ashamed. 'No wonder you look pale and stressed.'

'She's the cruelest person ever. Not just to me. To Dad, as well.'

'Was he with her yesterday?'

'No, but I've seen him, too. He looks so old and ill.'

'Oh, poor man … but I'm glad you've managed to see him. So it's not all bad, is it, dear? You've been missing him so much since you left home.'

It's incredible that Martha knows how much I've been missing him, but she's right. Seeing Dad twice in the past few days has made the empty space inside me hurt a bit less. I wonder when I'll see him again. I know it's up to me to make contact, but it's not as easy as it sounds.

Corvus keeps his unblinking eyes on me as I head for the stairs a few minutes later. He's not giving anything away, but I'm sure he knows everything about me, too! As I climb, I think how ridiculous it all is, believing he is somehow alive.

Martha has asked me to clean two of the rooms on the right. The first bedroom I tackle is like the other rooms. Ancient furniture, faded material, old-fashioned ornaments, dust, dust, dust. Martha could open her house as a museum. I bet she's had all this stuff since she was young, though she's so frail and wrinkled I can't imagine her as anything but an old woman.

As I go to the second bedroom door, I glance again along the corridor at the narrow set of stairs. If only I could quickly nip up there and sneak a peek in the room at the top of the turret. Mr J Bartrum's room, I presume. Perhaps Martha will ask me to clean up there when I've finished the rest of the house.

As soon as I push open the bedroom door, I notice a stunning wooden box on the dressing table in the window. It's about thirty by twenty centimetres and quite deep, very ornately decorated in gold with a mosaic peacock on the lid. I stand over it and stare. I'm aching with curiosity, but I refuse to touch it except with the duster. What does Martha keep in such a beautiful box?

'Are you ready for the party?' she asks, when I've finished my chores and we're sitting over our cup of tea.

'Almost.' I smile. 'But I'm going to have to be very cunning to get in without a ticket.'

I feel so relaxed with her now, and after a while I realise

I've been pouring out more memories of when I was a little girl.

'Sorry,' I say. 'I've talked too much. I must have tired you.'

'Oh no, dear. I love to hear about it. You were a happy little thing then, weren't you?'

I nod, close to tears. I would love to be 'a happy little thing' again.

Wednesday 8th December
Madebury

Dear Cecily
I haven't waited for your reply to my last letter as I know you'll be eager to know of my progress with Ella.

She's had a nasty experience since we last met, though it has nothing to do with the boy she's fallen for. It has something to do with her father's new wife, this dreadful woman Ella has made hints about before. I could see a shudder still remaining in the poor girl's shoulders when she arrived, so I set her to work straight away.

When she was done (and I am delighted with how bright

and shining my house is beginning to look), I got her talking about her childhood. You should have seen the difference those memories made to her demeanour.

Meanwhile, do you remember that box? That one father brought back from India? The one you've always admired, with the peacock on the lid? Well, I left it on the dressing table in one of the bedrooms that I set her to clean yesterday. I'm pleased with myself, for this is another mystery for her to wonder about. You are one of the few people who know what is inside the box. I'm sure Ella is as curious about it as I know she is about Jack.

But my clever plans don't end here. Did you doubt it? You know me too well, don't you? You will be delighted to hear that I have a few more surprises for my young prodigy. One of them will be tomorrow, another on Friday then several more on Saturday evening.

Do you know, I feel ten years younger since Ella landed in my life, well, more accurately, I suppose I landed in hers! I haven't felt my power so strongly for many, many years. It is truly exhilarating!

More news will follow shortly.
Your loving sister
Martha

25

The letter box rattles. It's still dark, but my clock tells me it's seven o'clock. No point in rushing downstairs to pick up the post. I never get any letters. No one knows where I live, so how could I? But even though I'm warm under my duvet, something draws me out of bed into the freezing cold of my room and down the stairs in my pyjamas. There are three letters. I pick them up. Two large ones are obviously trying to sell something. They'll get shoved straight in the recycling. The third is smaller, a cream-coloured envelope, I presume for one of the Snob Sisters.

But my heart flutters when I read my name, Ella Sharma, written in bold curly scrawl on the front. My hands shake so much I almost drop it. Who has written to me? Hurrying to the kitchen, I find a sharp knife and slit along the top. Inside is a single sheet of card and, as I pull it out and begin to read, I gasp and plonk myself down on the nearest chair. It's identical to the ones Bea and Tilly received, an invitation to Finn's party. Only this time the person invited is me!

I take deep breaths until I feel calmer. Once my shock has faded, I jump up and skip around the room, hugging the card to my chest and twirling round and round until I'm dizzy. I don't have to gate-crash. I have an invitation. I can go to the party!

I guess Finn didn't send it, nor his parents. They don't know who I am. So who else knows I'm desperate to go to the party?

Breathless and weak-kneed, I stop. It's Martha, of course. She knows everything about me. I've never told her my surname, yet it's written here. Her power over me has been getting stronger every day. It's almost as if she's planning my life, manipulating me.

I wonder if I should mind, but I don't ... I like it.

How did she manage to forge an invitation exactly like the others? And why is she doing all this for me? All I did was rescue her from a muddy pavement and take her home. Her thanks would have been enough.

I hear a sound, a creak on the stairs. I tuck the invitation and envelope in my pyjama pocket as the door opens.

'You're up early.' Velcro is wearing a thick dressing gown that reminds me of the one Dad used to wear. 'What are you doing?'

'Nothing.'

I've said it too quickly and he raises his eyebrows at me.

'Funny time of day to be doing nothing. You must be frozen. Here, wear this.' He goes to take off his dressing gown, but I leap to my feet. I don't want to get too cosy with him.

'I couldn't sleep … I was going to get some breakfast … '

'I'll make you some … go and get something warmer on and … '

'It's OK,' I say. 'I'm not really hungry now. Thanks anyway.'

Trying to ignore the disappointment on Velcro's face, I hurry from the kitchen. Back in my room I reread the invitation to make sure I haven't dreamed it, then I hide it in the shoe with the necklace and what's left of my money.

When I knock on Martha's door two hours later, she doesn't answer immediately. I wait and listen. I hear fluttering and a weird gargling sound from inside. I knock again and peer through the letter box. There is movement from the direction of the stairs, almost as if Corvus is on the move, but it's just out of my line of vision and I tell myself not to be so silly. I may have imagined he has winked at me a few times, but he is definitely firmly stuck in place on his newel post.

I don't know what to say to Martha when she finally comes to the door. I can't ask her about Corvus. Nor can I ask her point-blank about the invitation. I wait for her to tell me. But she doesn't. She spends her time nodding and muttering to herself and chuckling, so I begin to wonder if she has lost her marbles.

'Are you ready for the party?'

She has asked me that before. I frown and shake my head. I feel edgy.

I'm relieved when she sends me upstairs to work. I was hoping I might get a chance to climb the stairs to the turret, but I end up cleaning the bathroom and toilet. Next time, hopefully.

It's a few minutes to six when I reach work that evening. Hazel greets me with her usual frown, and I'm about to point out that I'm early for once when her hand jerks out from her side. I jump back, thinking she's going to hit me.

'Here,' she says. There is something in her hand. 'Take this. Though why I'm expected to be your messenger I'd really like to know.'

I reach forward and take it. 'Thanks.'

It's a small padded envelope with a white sticky label on the front. My name is typed on the label. Two envelopes in one day?

'You've got three minutes if you want to open it before you start work,' Hazel snaps.

Before she changes her mind, I rush across the lobby and dash through the doors. I need privacy. Quickly, I peel the end of the envelope open and pull out a small thin object wrapped in a single sheet of white paper. It's a mobile phone, a small, basic one – the kind I used to have before smartphones with apps and email came along. Its charger is inside the bag.

Puzzled, I unroll the sheet of paper and sit on the bottom of the stairs to read the note.

Dear Ella

    It's just a cheap phone so we can keep in touch. It's got £10 of calls on it. Please ring me at work when you can and I'll ring you back. Don't phone home!!

    Dad xx

    PS I miss you.

Dad! I bite my lip, fighting the tears, as Hazel bursts through the doors.

'Work starts right now,' she says.

I change into my overall, collect my mop and bucket and climb the stairs. I'll ring Dad before I go to Martha's in the morning.

26

I've still got loads of energy when I leave work. I feel upbeat. I wonder if it's because of Dad, or Martha, or the fact that I'm going to the party. I decide it must be a combination of all those things.

It's a cold, starlit evening and there's a full moon. I'm wearing my trainers so I decide to go for a jog. I know exactly where I'll go, my usual route up to Kestrel Rise. Finn's house is lit up like the Christmas lights in Oxford Street and the security light shows me a shiny new red Mini Coupé parked in the drive. I dodge behind a parked car opposite as the front door opens.

Then my heart almost stops. Finn rushes out, gets in the driver's seat and starts the engine. Could this car be his? An eighteenth birthday present from his parents? He revs the engine for a few moments then turns it off. Getting out, he stands looking at the car. The muscles in his arms ripple as he closes the door. In two days' time I'll be in those arms.

I stay there until Finn goes inside, then I jog back along the road and down the hill. I pass Bella Casa café, which looks busy even at this time of night, along the High Street, through groups of people on their way home, past Luigi's, all in darkness, to the corner of Martha's road.

I stop and bend, hands on knees, to catch my breath. As I straighten up I'm aware of a shadow coming fast from the High Street. The shadow collides with me and I land with a thud on the cold ground.

'Sorry!' Before I can judge whether I'm hurt or not, I feel hands tugging me back onto my feet. 'Are you all right?'

Although I'm shaken and think I may have a grazed knee, I nod, struck dumb. In the glow from the street lamp, I've just recognised him. He's just like his photo.

It's Mr J Bartrum. He bends to peer at me and I can just make out a smile.

'I'm fine, thanks.'

'Sorry,' he says again. 'I didn't see you.'

'It was my fault. I shouldn't have stopped right there.'

'Well, if you're sure you're OK … '

'Yes.'

I turn to go. I'm confused and embarrassed. He's really nice. I know who he is, but I'm sure he doesn't know who I am. I bet Martha hasn't even told him she gets a visitor every day while he's out at work. If I talk to him, I might let her secret out.

'Bye,' we both say together.

I turn back and watch him jog all the way to Martha's.

Half an hour later, I lie tossing in my bed. How can I sleep? I'm reliving everything that has happened. Until a short while ago my life was so empty and miserable and now suddenly, everything is different. And it's all since I met Martha.

I don't dream when I eventually drop off to sleep, and when I wake, my first thought is that it is Friday. One more day. It's going to be some party. And I keep pinching myself. It's so incredible. I'm going to be there!

I put my surprise meeting with Mr J to the back of my mind as I list what I need to do:

1. Go to Martha's. I hope I'll feel less embarrassed than last time, as we had been getting on so brilliantly.
2. See if I can find jewellery in the shops … a necklace, earrings and a hair clasp.
3. I might go to Luigi's.
4. Go to work at six, but even that isn't all bad as it's payday.
5. But first, I'll ring Dad. Do I feel nervous about it? Yes, very. Best get it out of the way.

Sitting on my bed, I open up my new mobile and dial his work number. Brenda answers almost immediately and she chirrups away when she recognises my voice.

'He told me you might call. And Ella, I know it's none of my business, but I'm so glad you've got in touch. He's looking better already, though he did seem rather tense again this morning when he arrived.'

She doesn't say any more about that, but I'm hoping it means he's having a bad time at home. Not that I want him to suffer, but perhaps he really is recognising the huge mistake he's made getting hitched to that creature. There are several clicks and then Dad's on the line.

'Thanks for the mobile,' I say. I feel shy, as if I don't really know him.

'I did it for me.' I can hear the smile in his voice, one that he used to have a long time ago. 'I wanted to give you the means to ring me.'

'I'm glad you did.'

'Are you, Ella? Really?'

'Mmm.'

I feel his smile broadening and mine matches it.

'Lunch today?'

I shouldn't have hesitated, but I'm trying to work out my schedule. I desperately want to see him again, but I'm not sure how much time I'll have between Martha's and the jewellery shops.

'Not if you don't want to.' His voice has lost its cheerfulness.

It gives me a jolt. I mean that much to him.

'Of course I want to. What time? Where?'

'It's a fine day. Wrap up warm and let's meet in that park just behind your office block. We'll have a picnic, shall we?'

'Lovely.'

'I'll get Brenda to buy a few things. Shall we say one o'clock near the bandstand?'

'Yes. Great.'

When we have rung off I feel soothed as if I'm wrapped in a comfort blanket. I hum as I get ready for my visit to Martha's. I pull my money from the shoe and put it in my purse. I'll take it with me, then I can go straight on the jewellery hunt after lunch with Dad.

Martha still has her mischievous twinkle as she steps back for me to enter her house, but Corvus glares at me. He seems almost as alarming as he did the first time we met. It's like he's giving me a warning. I wonder what I've done.

Martha asks me to clean the windows in the downstairs rooms. They take longer than I expect because they are so covered in grime they need polishing several times to make them sparkle. I'm pleased with my effort and I've just finished in the study, where I take another good look at Mr J's photo, when the door opens and Martha comes into the room.

Glancing around, she nods, smiles then beckons to me. She says nothing and I follow her to the kitchen.

'Sit down a moment,' she says. 'I want to talk to you.'

27

Martha's face has changed, as if she has wiped the brightness from her eyes. She has become serious. I tense up as we sit down opposite each other in our usual chairs. It's almost like I've been summoned to the head teacher's room. Then Martha begins to fidget as if *she's* the impatient child. I'm trying to work out what is coming, whether she's going to sack me or blame me for something I haven't done. I stay silent, gripping my hands together under the table, my shoulders painful with tension.

Martha takes a deep gulping breath then speaks. 'Do you remember seeing an ornate wooden box when you were cleaning upstairs yesterday, dear?'

At least she has called me 'dear'. I can't have done anything too dreadful.

'The one with the beautiful peacock on the lid?'

'Yes. Go and fetch it for me, will you?'

Glad of the excuse to leave the table, I jump up and almost run along the corridor. I dodge round Corvus, who seems to have grown bigger in the few minutes since I last saw him. Leaping up the stairs two at a time, I reach the bedroom door and gently push it open. The box is exactly where it was before. I tiptoe across the room like a thief and, putting one hand each side, lift it. It's quite heavy so my journey downstairs is much slower. I stop at the bottom.

'What's going on?' I whisper to Corvus, but he doesn't respond except to give me a hard stare. I'm disappointed. Until this morning, I thought we were beginning to get on rather well.

I hurry to the kitchen and place the box in the middle of the table.

'Thank you.' Martha reaches out and touches the peacock with the tips of her fingers. My mouth opens and closes like a fish as the peacock glows in the dull light of the room.

'Do you know what's inside this box?'

I shake my head, unsure whether she is testing me again or just asking a simple question.

'Of course you don't, although I expect you're curious about it, as you are about several things you have seen in this house?'

I nod, silenced by the tension that is still gripping me. Her face breaks into a little smile then she grows serious again.

'Well, let's see, shall we?' She reaches out and is about to lift the lid, then stops, her hand hovering. 'Are you ready for your party tomorrow?'

I can't understand why she has asked me for a third time or why she has changed the subject so abruptly.

'Not quite.'

She peers at me, her hand remaining a few centimetres above the peacock, which glows brighter than ever. She is waiting for me to say more.

'I … I've got the dress, of course, thanks to you … I've got an invitation … that's a mystery … and I've bought some shoes, but … '

' … but you need jewellery.'

As she speaks, she tips the lid open. I flinch at the flickering brightness from inside the box, which she pushes towards me. I peer in, then look up into her eyes. The twinkle is almost as bright as the contents of the box. She has been teasing me again. I try to smile, but I'm unsure of how I'm supposed to react.

'Well?' Her head is on one side, birdlike. 'Will they do?'

'What … what do you mean?'

She reaches in the box and lifts out the most gorgeous necklace I've ever seen. I stare, open-mouthed. It's just like the one I've dreamt about, a delicate chain of feathers, each feather patterned with tiny white stones. I'm sure these must be real diamonds. Mum would have absolutely loved it. And so do I!

'Would you like to borrow it tomorrow night?'

'But … '

Martha beams and hands the necklace over. I swallow hard as I drape it over the back of my hand.

'It looks perfect against your skin,' she says.

I don't know what to say. She is right. The diamonds contrast so well with my brown hand.

'I'm sure you'll like these, too.' She lifts out a pair of matching earrings that glisten as she dangles them in front of me.

'They're gorgeous.'

She hands them to me. 'And I presume for such an occasion you will put your hair up?' she asks.

I nod, wondering for the hundredth time how she knows exactly what I've been thinking.

'So you'll need this.' Her hand delves into the box for a third time and pulls out a hair clasp that matches the necklace and earrings.

'Why don't you try them on?'

With clumsy fingers I fasten the necklace at the back of my neck and hook the earrings through my ears. Then I sweep my hair onto the top of my head and fasten it in place with the clasp.

'Beautiful!' she gasps. 'There's a mirror in the hall. Go and take a look at yourself. See what you think.'

I stare at myself in the mirror. In spite of my old clothes, I look a completely different person. Martha's magic is working really strongly. I can feel it through the jewellery, seeping through my body. It makes me feel great.

At that moment, I start and whip round. I've heard a faint noise that I'm certain came from Corvus. It sounded like, 'You'll do.'

I face him, hands on hips, but he doesn't give anything

more away. Most witches in stories have a cat as their assistants. There doesn't seem to be anything magical about the cat that's always in the front garden. Perhaps it isn't even Martha's. No, my good witch has a stuffed raven!

'Well?' Martha asks when I get back to the kitchen.

'They're all beautiful,' I say. 'And they make me look kind of different.'

'Of course.' Martha gives the biggest smile yet.

'I hardly recognised myself.'

'So would you like to borrow them?'

My brain is in turmoil. 'I'd *love* to,' I whisper as I pull out the clasp and let my hair drop, 'but I'd be terrified of losing them.'

'Don't worry, dear. They will be quite safe.'

I don't argue, but I wonder how she can be so confident. I take off the earrings and unfasten the necklace. Martha walks slowly to a cupboard and takes out a much smaller box, which she brings to the table. The jewellery just fits inside it.

'Well, if you're sure,' I whisper. I gently give her a hug. 'Thank you.'

'My pleasure.' She is beaming at me, as if her kindness really is giving her pleasure.

'Martha, why are you doing all this for me?'

She doesn't answer for a moment. Her eyes become misty and she seems to be looking at something far away.

'It's a long story,' she says eventually. 'Maybe I'll tell it to you one day … oh, and one more thing … I've arranged for your taxi to pick you up at eight-thirty tomorrow night. Is that all right?'

'Yes … and thank you.'

Ten minutes later, I'm opening the front door with the box tucked inside my backpack. I glance over my shoulder at Corvus. He stares at the backpack then gives me a knowing look.

'I promise I'll look after the jewels,' I say, and I'm sure he nods.

Friday 10th December
Madebury

Dear Cecily
I can hardly contain my excitement. Everything is going to plan and Ella is responding so well to my attentions. She reminds me so much of myself when I was her age. I realise you're the only person on this earth who knows my story, but I won't go into all that now. Since that time, of course, my fortunes have changed incredibly. I'm determined Ella's will, too.

She looked stunning in my diamonds. I've lent them to her — the necklace, earrings and hair clasp. She was genuinely shocked when I asked if she would like to borrow them. I know you'll be furious with me, but I'm certain they are in safe hands. Corvus will make sure they don't come to any harm. He is playing his part excellently and is ready for action. Tomorrow is the big day.

Jack has started noticing changes in the house. I didn't think he would. He's such an idle fellow. But he asked me if I was tired last evening before he went out for a run. When I queried why he had asked, he said I must have been working hard to make the place look so clean. Cheeky boy! If he'd noticed the dust previously he could have done some cleaning himself, but I know he works very hard in his job so I'll let him off. It's about time I told him about my little visitor, I think.

Ella left very promptly today. I wondered if I had overwhelmed her with the loan of the jewels and the promise of a taxi, but I also had the feeling she was meeting someone. She hasn't told me anything more about herself lately. In fact, she's been quieter than usual. I hope desperately that I haven't upset her by foisting these things upon her. Does she realise it was me who sent her an invitation to the party, I wonder?

I am awaiting the outcome of all this with great anticipation. Tomorrow night will be a test of everything. I will keep you informed as usual.

Your loving sister
Martha

28

Dad is waiting for me when I arrive at the park. He's in the bandstand, a sad lonely figure sitting with his head in his hands, a supermarket bag at his feet. He brightens up when he sees me coming and lopes down the steps to meet me, hugs me tightly and kisses my cheek. Such a difference to when I met him in the Chinese restaurant.

'Where shall we go?' he asks.

'Why don't we stay here?' I say, looking up at the sky. 'I think it's going to rain.'

The wind whips across the park as we huddle together on the curved seat that runs around the inside of the bandstand. I put my backpack safely under the seat, only too aware of what is inside it. He opens the poly bag and pulls out the lunch Brenda has bought for us. I notice straight away that his hands are shaking and the smile that lit up his face as he greeted me has faded. His eyes are sunk in deep dark hollows.

'Dad, are you all right?'

He flashes a false smile. 'Of course, why wouldn't I be?'

I can't explain my fear that the tyrant of a wife is making him ill. I bite my sandwich while I think of what to say. He coughs and takes a deep breath as if he is about to speak, then thinks better of it and stares out across the park.

'Eat up!' I say, too brightly.

He looks at me and I'm sure there are tears in his eyes.

'Do you know, you look so much like your mother did when I first met her,' he says.

'But she was fair and I'm dark like you,' I say.

He nods. 'It's your mannerisms,' he says. 'The way you brush your hair away from your face; the way you smile.'

I reach out and touch his arm and he grasps my hand. I find I'm crying, but then I sniff back the tears. I don't want to show too much feeling, not straight away. After all, he did nothing to stop Sonia throwing me out. I still have to learn to forgive him for that.

'We need to talk.' He glances around like a spy in a conspiracy, but there is no one near. It's raining steadily now and just a few hardy dog walkers are passing in the distance.

We eat in silence for a few minutes. My stomach is churning with nerves, but I force the food down.

At last, he swallows and folds his arms.

'I loved your mother so much,' he says. 'And when she died the world almost came to an end for me … if it hadn't been for you, Ella … ' He bites his lip.

I bite mine.

'We managed, you and I, didn't we?'

I nod.

'Then, out of the blue, came a brightness that seemed to sweep away a lot of my sadness.'

I don't need him to explain what he's getting at and I don't interrupt.

'Sonia had been around for a while, of course, your mum's friend. But when I met up with her soon after ... ' He paused and I could see he was trying to stay calm. ' ... I suddenly realised she was witty, attractive, lively ... she was fun to be with.'

I notice how he is using the past tense. She *was* fun to be with. Not *is*.

'But things change.' He sighs. 'I'm so sorry, Ella.'

I know he has seen the raptor in her. Her talons that were ripping me to shreds are doing the same to him.

'So what are you going to do?' I whisper.

'I don't know. I have to tread so carefully.' He looks at his watch and shakes himself, as if to bring himself back to the present. 'I've got to go. I have a board meeting in half an hour.'

I wish we could stay here much longer, but I know he's always busy at work.

'It's lovely to see you, Dad.'

He smiles. 'And you ... you're looking very pretty.'

I return the smile. Dads are allowed to say that kind of thing. 'Strange things have been happening ... '

'A boy?'

'Partly.' I feel the heat rise to my face. 'But ... ' How can

I admit that I'm completely smitten with a boy I've never really met? How can I explain about Martha and her magic? Next time I see Dad I might try.

We pack away the rubbish and stand up. Holding my backpack tightly, I walk with him to his car and we hug each other for ages. It's as if we're clinging to each other for comfort.

'Oh, I almost forgot to tell you,' he says, 'when you ... left home ... several of your friends came to the house, asking after you.'

'What did you tell them?'

'I didn't get a chance to say anything. Sonia saw them all off and they haven't been back.'

No prizes for guessing why!

As Dad drives off, I wave then turn back towards town. I wish he would escape from Sonia's grip as I'm sure he wants to, but I bet she's dug her talons in so deep he'll have terrible trouble shaking her off.

I walk from the car park, deep in my thoughts. I suppose it was easy for Dad to guess I'm in love. I've probably got Finn's name written across my forehead!

Finn. I've been so stunned by Martha's kindness and Dad's misery that I've let him fade from my mind for most of the day. I can soon make up for that, though. As I walk, a vision of his face, his hair, his eyes comes back strongly. On Saturday night, all my dreams will come true. I'll let thoughts of Finn take me over from now on.

Of course I don't need to search for jewellery now, so I go back to my room and chill out for a couple of hours before I go to work. I feel drained, exhausted by an odd mixture of sadness, excitement and bewilderment. The last few weeks have passed in such a whirlwind. I can't help wondering what's going to happen next.

And I suspect Martha hasn't finished with me yet.

29

'Hey, Jodie!'

'Ella! Is that really you?' Her voice squeals so loudly I have to hold the mobile away from my ear. 'Where are you? Where've you been all this time? Are you all right?' She sounds almost hysterical as she fires a long string of questions at me. I wait until she pauses for breath. But then I find I can't answer any of her questions. I don't know where to begin.

'Ella? Are you still there?'

'Yes.'

I can't believe I'm so tongue-tied with my friend. Only a few weeks ago, we hardly ever stopped nattering when we were together … got into trouble for it so many times at school. 'I'm OK. Only I can't explain it all now.'

'Why haven't you rung me before?'

'I lost my phone.'

'There's such a thing as a call box … '

'I know, but … '

'Don't you realise how worried we've been? You could have warned us you were going to disappear. I've had to lie … '

'Thanks. I'm really grateful, Jodie … but I had to get right away in a hurry. You wouldn't understand … '

'Wouldn't I just? It was that … that … *monster* your dad married, wasn't it? I can't imagine having her for a step-mother. She gave me such an earful … '

'I know,' I say. 'Dad told me.'

'You've seen your dad? Thank gawd for that. My dad said he thought yours was about to have a breakdown … "Poor man," he says, "being married to that harridan after such a lovely wife died … then his daughter disappearing … " '

'He knew why I went,' I snap. Why should I have to justify my actions to Jodie? 'I left him a note and told him roughly where I was going. But he didn't seem to care. He was too besotted.'

'Don't get me wrong. I'm not blaming you. It's so brilliant to hear your voice. Where are you? Can we meet up and chat?'

That's what I've been hoping she would say. I'll be able to tell her all about Finn and the party … *after* the party.

'Not yet. Next week? I've got so much to tell you.'

'But Ella … '

'Look, I've got to go. Not much time left on my phone.'

'I could ring you back.' It sounds like she's pleading with me.

'I'll text you.'
'Promise?'
'Promise … Bye.'
I press the red button then turn off the phone.

30

When I wake up on Saturday morning, I instantly feel such a fluttering in my stomach I know I won't be able to eat anything. I go downstairs when I'm showered and dressed and find Velcro in the kitchen as usual. I haven't told anyone, even him, about getting the invitation, but he's been so kind to me, I don't want to keep him in the dark any longer. Besides, I need to share it with someone.

Sitting down at the table, I pull the envelope from my pocket and thrust it under his nose.

'What's this?'

'Have a look.'

He takes the envelope and pulls out the card. His pale eyebrows rise as he reads. 'How come?' he asks. 'I thought you didn't know him.'

I've been thinking about how I can explain it. For better or worse, now it's time to tell all.

'It arrived a few days ago … I'm sure it wasn't from Finn … but … well, do you remember that old lady I told you about?'

He nods. 'What about her?'

'Well, I think she sent it … '

'You're winding me up.'

'I'm not … there's something magical about her and … '

'Get real,' he says.

'I'm serious, Velcro. I felt it as soon as I met her. Then there's her raven, Corvus. I'm sure he's not just a stuffed bird, and … '

'Ella. Are you on something?'

I shake my head. 'And Martha knew which dress I wanted … that black one … and my size … and she bought it for me. And she knows about Finn. In fact I think she had something to do with me fancying him. I mentioned his party to her one day and how I'd love to go and I think she must have forged this invitation and sent it.'

'You've gone crazy.'

I feel my eyes welling up. 'I would have told you before, but I guessed you'd say something like that.'

I stand up. I was going to tell him about the jewellery as well, but dash from the room before I burst into tears. I meet Tilly on the landing, but she hardly notices me. She knocks on Bea's bedroom door and barges in. I hear them chirruping away like a couple of high-class sparrows as I go into my room.

A few minutes later, there's a light tap on my door.

I check myself in the mirror before going to open it. I guess it's Velcro and I don't want him to know I've been blubbing. He stands there, leaning against the doorframe, smiling.

'Sorry, Ella, I didn't mean to upset you.'

I step back, letting him in. We sit down side by side on my bed.

'You must admit, what you told me is a bit bizarre,' he says, 'but I take back what I said about you being crazy. I suppose there must be something extraordinary about that old lady.'

I feel the shiver of a sigh pass through my body. 'Thanks.'

'So you don't need to gate-crash the party now.'

'No.'

He's so kind. It's a pity I didn't fall for him! But he's not my type, in the romantic sense … just a good friend.

Later that morning, I go for a jog. It helps calm my nerves and passes the time. I take my usual route, up the hill to Finn's house. There's no sign of him or his parents, so I jog back down the hill, along the High Street and turn the corner into Martha's road. I wonder if I'll meet Mr J again, but he doesn't appear. I'm amazed to find I feel disappointed.

When I get home, I have a sudden urge to phone Dad, but I daren't. Not at home on a Saturday. I couldn't face a lashing from that woman's tongue. So I go down to the lounge and mindlessly watch TV. Velcro likes old films and the one we watch isn't as bad as I expected.

Tilly and Bea spend much of the day preening

themselves. Bea becomes even blonder and Tilly deepens the copper tones in her hair. They both paint their fingernails and toenails to match their dresses, and spend hours experimenting with the most flattering make-up. They pop into the lounge from time to time to demand that I do something for them – or occasionally to ask my opinion. I obey without complaining, then say the right things and they go away pleased with their appearance.

'Aren't you going to get ready?' Velcro asks as the film ends.

'Not yet. It won't take me long. Anyway, I don't want those two to know I'm going to the party. I'll wait till they've gone before I make my move.'

Make my move? I wonder what that move will bring.

By seven o'clock, the Snob Sisters are at their most demanding.

'Ella, bring me my dress.'

'Ella, where are my shoes?'

'Ella, brush my hair.'

For an hour, it's 'Ella this', 'Ella that', with not one 'Please' or 'Thank you', but at least it keeps me busy and stops the nerves that are bubbling away just below the surface.

At last, they are ready. They both look stunning, I have to admit. And I know they're both after Finn. I'll just have to hope neither of them gets their hands on him before I arrive. Then, with squeaks and squawks, they are in the taxi and gone. I wave them off, but they've already forgotten about me. They're so full of themselves and who will make the all-important conquest.

31

After I've closed the door, Velcro follows me upstairs.

'Want any help?' he asks.

'I might do. Just let me get my make-up done and my dress on, then I'll call you.'

I sit at my dressing table in my underwear and stare at the dark-eyed girl in the mirror. She won't attract anybody looking like that. She needs a miracle.

After heavy eye-liner and mascara, deep pink lip gloss and a touch of blusher on my brown cheeks, I see the beginnings of the transformation.

I'm on Mum's lap, book open, the story just begun. I'm looking at the pictures, listening to her voice, so full of expression as she reads. It's my favourite story and she has read it to me hundreds of times. She must be sick of it, but she doesn't show that. The ending is the best part, when the ugly duckling becomes a beautiful swan.

I step into the black dress and wriggle as I pull up the zip. Then I slip on the shoes. They're higher than I've ever had before, but my need to look elegant and impress the only person I'm interested in will make any discomfort worthwhile. I look at myself in the long wardrobe mirror. The black swan! I go to my door and call. Velcro appears immediately. He must have been waiting close by.

'Wow!' That's all he can manage as he watches me brush my hair.

Martha's box is on the bed. I take it to the dressing table, open it and pull out the hair clasp. Velcro's eyes widen when he sees it, but he doesn't say anything. Putting it down for a moment, I twist my hair up on top of my head. I've been practising this since Martha gave me the clasp, but now my hands are shaking and I can't get it right.

'Let me.'

I hadn't thought of Velcro as a hairdresser, but I soon find he has the knack. He nips along the landing and returns with some of Bea's hair gear. In no time, with the help of a few invisible hairpins, some big volume mousse and a few squirts of lacquer, my hair is up in a fabulous swirl.

'Where do you want this?' Velcro asks, picking up the clasp.

Together we find the best place for it, behind my left ear, where it clips into place. It's the finishing touch needed to hold my hair securely. Its feathery pattern of diamonds dazzles, glistening against my black hair.

I reach in the box again and lift out the earrings.

'They look like real diamonds,' Velcro says.

I smile and push them through the holes in my ear lobes. I gently toss my head and watch them flutter like tiny bird wings. 'They *are* real diamonds,' I say.

When I bring out the necklace and fasten it at the back of my neck, Velcro's face is full of worry lines. 'Where did you get all these from? They must be worth a fortune. You didn't steal them, did you?'

I can forgive him for asking. He knows about the incident in the department store, so he's allowed to have his doubts, but I put on a hurt expression.

'Sorry,' he says, 'but you've made a big thing about being poor … '

'I *am* poor.'

'But … ?'

'Martha lent them to me.'

'Blimey! I thought all that about the dress and the ticket was enough, but this … well, you've certainly made a hit with her!'

Martha promised the taxi for eight-thirty. It's almost that now. I stand up and parade about in front of Velcro.

'You look amazing,' he sighs. 'And beautiful.'

'Thanks.' I know he means it.

'Are you sure you want to throw yourself away on an arrogant prig like Finn?'

I don't respond to that. There's no point in getting into an embarrassing discussion now. 'I'm ready,' I say.

'Haven't you got a coat?'

'No, only my old one and I can't wear that. I'll be all right. It's not so cold tonight.'

I pick up my bag, checking my phone and the invitation are inside, and as we go downstairs there is a gentle tap on the front door. A dark shadow moves behind the opaque glass. I hurry to open the door.

Standing there is the strangest man I've ever seen. He's dressed in a black shiny suit and peculiar sharp black shoes, but I can't stop staring at his face. With his jet-black sleeked-back hair, slate-grey eyes and enormous pointed nose, he looks exactly like Corvus!

'Your carriage awaits, Ma'am,' he says, sounding like he's got a cheese grater in his throat.

I hesitate, not sure about this mysterious relationship I have with the raven. Perhaps I *am* going crazy.

'You'll do,' he mutters. I've heard him say that once before. Then he winks and I know it's him. And I'm certain Martha would not have sent him if she didn't trust him. Now I understand why she said Corvus would make sure the jewels were safe.

'Good luck,' Velcro whispers as I follow the strange man outside, but I know he doesn't mean it. Not where Finn is concerned anyway.

Corvus leads me to a weird-looking car. It looks a bit like a large, orange bubble. He opens the rear door and bows, his nose almost touching the ground, as I climb in. His driving is as strange as the rest of him, more like soaring and swooping than driving, but we arrive at the manor in one piece. The car circles twice in the wide gravel area in front of a grand flight of stone steps, then we glide to a halt. Bright lights shine from every window of the manor and I hear the beat of music as soon as Corvus opens the car door for me.

I'm shivering, not from the night air, but more likely from the shock of the car ride and my nerves, which are jangling at the thought of making an entrance at the party.

'I will return for you just before midnight, Ma'am,' croaks Corvus. 'Be sure to be ready before the witching hour. I cannot wait a second later than the first stroke of twelve.'

'Thank you,' I say as I mount the steps. 'I'll be here.'

The car zooms away and, when I reach the top and turn, it has already disappeared into the darkness.

32

Shaking off the bizarre experience with Corvus, I turn back towards the Manor. I realise I'm trembling and part of me wants to run away. How can I just breeze in and join in the party?

I could easily walk home along the lanes and forget the whole thing, but my desire to be in the arms of Finn draws me in. Anyway, I can't let Martha down after all the help she's given me.

Pushing open the heavy wooden door, I tiptoe inside. Blinking in the brilliance of the lights in the grand entrance hall, I show my invitation to a bouncer by the door – and I'm in! A legitimate gate-crasher! I find the Ladies to check that my extraordinary journey hasn't ruined my appearance and I'm amazed at the reflection that smiles back at me. Is that really me?

I head towards the noise and slide into a massive room where girls in stunning outfits and guys in smart gear are bobbing and gyrating to the rhythm of the music. Through the crowds I can make out a band at the far end. There are tall French windows all along one side, balloons and lights and decorations strung across the room, and a bar along the wall opposite the windows. I can't see Finn.

I'm skirting round the edge of the dancers towards the bar when someone lurches in front of me. I just have time to glimpse the flash of a red dress and long blonde hair before I'm standing face to face with Bea.

'Oops, sorry,' she mouths, then lurches away. She hasn't recognised me.

Feeling slightly more confident, I reach the bar and get a coke. I stand for a long time with my back to the wall, sipping my drink, giving myself time to relax and take it all in. Everyone seems to be having a great time, but there's still no sign of Finn.

My eyes scour the room. Then a gap appears in the crowd and I see him. He's dancing with a tall, willowy girl in a weird yellow dress like a feathery tutu. It looks as if she's auditioning for the part of a duckling. My heart tightens as his arms wrap around her and he pulls her roughly towards him.

I close my eyes. She can't have him. He's mine.

When I look again, they are gone, lost in the middle of the mob, but a few minutes later I catch sight of his golden hair. He's still dancing, this time with a copper-haired girl. It's Tilly. She's got her hands on him, as she promised. It's time I made a move.

I try pushing through, but it's too crowded. There are too many stomping feet that threaten to crush mine and too many sharp elbows that prod me like a hedge of thorns surrounding him, keeping me away. I try dancing, mingling with the crowds, but I can't get near him. Each time I see him, he's with a different girl. I tell myself that's to be expected. He *is* gorgeous and it *is* his birthday party. Everyone wants to dance with him. But when he gets a chance to see me, he'll forget everyone else. At least, that's what I'm hoping.

Someone touches my arm. 'Fancy a dance?'

I shrug. 'OK.' No point in refusing. I don't really notice who he is or what he looks like. I'm too busy concentrating on looking out for Finn. I just let the music take me.

The time seems to flash by as I dance. Then all of a sudden, I notice it's almost eleven by the big clock on the wall. I'm beginning to panic. I've got to leave in an hour and I haven't even had a chance to get close to him.

Tilly and Bea have both passed near me several times, but neither of them recognised me. They're making fools of themselves. I bet they've had too much to drink! Their dresses are too short and they're too loud, squealing and squawking against the volume of the music.

I'm standing by the bar with another coke in my hand when suddenly he's there, even taller than I'd imagined, towering over me, his deep brown eyes boring into mine. I almost drop the glass.

'Well, hi!' he yells.

My heart racing, I let him take my glass and put it down on the bar.

'Where have *you* been all my life?'

I cringe at his old-fashioned cliché, but forgive him. I'd forgive him anything. He reaches for me and draws me into his arms. I've dared to dream of this moment ever since I first set eyes on him.

'You're beautiful,' he yells into my ear, as he guides me through the mass of bodies into the middle of the room. He whirls me round and round. I'm dizzy with passion for him. The room, dancers, lights, music, everything disappears. We're on our own. Nothing else matters. I'm in heaven.

The band stops. The dance is over. I hold my breath. Was that it? Will Finn find another girl for the next dance? But I don't have to worry. He holds my hand and looks down at me with such an amorous expression I think I'm going to faint. The music begins again. It goes on and on, with the two of us moving in time.

Suddenly, as he pulls me tight into his chest, an unpleasant smell wafts up my nose. I sniff. It's body odour. It's pretty strong and it isn't me. It's Finn.

I move my head backwards slightly so I can breathe something fresher, but he pulls me closer. I'm so much smaller than him that I find my nose pushed right into his chest. I persuade myself it's because it's like a sauna inside the room. He's been dancing all evening so he's bound to be sweating, but I can't stand it for long.

'It's so hot in here!' I yell. 'I need air!'

He grins, more like a leer really. 'Thought you'd never ask!' Another cliché! 'Let's go out on the balcony.'

He grabs my hand and tugs me towards the nearest

French window. We pass Bea and Tilly, who watch with envious looks in their eyes, but it's obvious they still don't know who I am.

Outside on the balcony, in the dark, I gasp in the cold air, relieved I've got away from the whiff of Finn's body odour, but immediately he's full on, at point-blank range, breathing heavily on me. I'm taken over by another smell. His breath is foul.

Then, before I can react, he's shoved me against the wall. His lips have locked onto mine and he's all over me, thrusting his knee between my legs, his hands exploring my body, his probing tongue down my throat. He has taken me completely by surprise and, as if by magic, my adoration for him disappears.

Martha's spell is broken.

I struggle, but he's too strong and, as he yanks at my dress, I know I'm helpless. Like a blow in the stomach, I realise what I should have seen straight away. He's nothing but a self-opinionated letch.

My dream has fast become a nightmare. I blame myself for being naïve. I was simply thinking of him as my golden boy. I'd been looking for old-fashioned romance with a big 'R'.

'Hey, Finn.' A voice comes out of the darkness. 'Put the girl down. Can't you see she's not enjoying it?'

Finn lets go as swiftly as he grabbed me and I almost collapse onto the floor of the balcony. He swears loudly and obscenely, foul-mouthing whoever disturbed him, and shoots back into the house. I turn to thank my rescuer, then gasp. He looks very different, dressed smartly instead of in his running

Saturday 11th December
Madebury

Dear Cecily
    It's almost ten o'clock on a Saturday evening. I should be in bed by now, but I'm too restless to sleep.
    I know you'll forgive me for writing again so soon. I can't keep everything to myself. My excitement is intense. My heart is racing in anticipation. I do hope I'm not making myself ill over this.
    Of course, you know what I'm talking about. At this moment, I hope that young Ella is in the arms of the young man

she has fallen in love with. Apart from the fact that he wasn't quite my choice for her, my magic has worked well so far. I do hope everything goes according to her dreams and wishes.

Corvus reports that Ella arrived safely at her destination and she promised him she would be ready to leave before midnight. You know how important that is in the tradition of magic, so I hope she keeps her promise.

A few days ago, I discovered that young Jack was invited to the same party. Apparently, he met the object of Ella's desires several times at the gymnasium. So he, too, had an invitation. However, Ella and Jack have never met, so they won't recognise each other. Or maybe she will know who he is. As I said before, she has seen his photo.

You won't receive this letter until well after the party is over, of course, as the post won't go until Monday morning, but I just had to write to release some of my excitement. I just hope my magic continues to work well and that the outcome of all of this means a great deal of happiness for dear Ella.

I will write again when I know the outcome.

Your loving sister

Martha

PS I am about to set in motion one more project in connection with this. Something needs to be done about that dreadful woman who is the cause of much of Ella's misery.

33

My rescuer is watching me from the shadows.

'Thanks,' I mumble when I can get my breath. I straighten my dress. I'm still shaking and I feel my burning face growing hotter as I try to work out whether he has recognised me from our couple of meetings in the street. Tilly and Bea have no idea who I am, so I presume he hasn't either.

He shrugs. 'That's OK,' he says. 'I know what Finn's like. I saw him drag you out here.'

I shudder. So Finn already has a reputation. I know I should have guessed, but my infatuation for him must have stopped me. I totter and reach for the wall.

'Are you all right?'

I meet his gaze. I've heard him say that before, when he knocked me down on the corner of Martha's road. I wonder if it rings bells in his mind, too. I nod and force a smile, though I don't feel very cheerful after my experience with Finn.

'I'm Jack.'

Jack. So now I know! I wonder if Martha has told him about me.

'I'm Ella.'

'Anything I can do to help, Ella?'

'No, I'll find the Ladies and … ' My hand brushes against my ear. I squeal, heart pounding in fear.

'What?'

'My earring. I've lost an earring!' I touch my neck, hair and other ear. Nothing else is missing, but to lose any of Martha's jewellery is disastrous.

'It must have fallen off when Finn had you in that clinch.'

We scrabble around together on the floor searching every centimetre of the balcony, but can't find it anywhere. At that moment, I hear a distant church bell.

'What's the time?'

Jack looks at his watch. 'Midnight.'

I fight back tears. Everything has gone wrong. First Finn, then the earring, and now I've broken my promise to Corvus.

'Don't worry, we'll find the earring,' says Jack. 'I'll go and ferret out Finn. It might be hooked on his clothes.' He hurries inside.

Startled by a scraping sound, I look up. Sitting on the balustrade of the balcony is a large black bird. Dangling from his beak is something feathery and shiny. It's the earring.

'Corvus,' I whisper. 'Thanks goodness you've found it.'

I reach out, but the raven winks, flaps his wings and takes off into the night.

'Making sure the jewellery comes to no harm,' I mutter, then I slip back into the house, and creep round the edge of the room. I'm convinced that everybody will stare at me, but the dancing is more frenetic than ever and I reach the door unnoticed. I meet nobody in the entrance hall and quietly let myself out of the manor.

There is no sign of the car or the chauffeur. I didn't expect there to be. Corvus obviously changed back into a raven on the stroke of midnight. I'll have to walk.

Scuttling along the lanes alone in high heels in the pitch dark isn't much fun and my feet are killing me. I dodge into the hedgerow each time a car shoots by. I don't want to be picked up by a pervert or murderer. So when one of the cars slows down behind me I'm petrified and my legs don't want to obey my brain. The car stops. I freeze inside, but manage to stumble on.

'Ella!' It's Jack.

I stop, but don't turn round. My long shadow tells me I'm caught in his headlights.

'Ella, I guessed you'd legged it.' His tone is gentle, persuasive. 'I'll take you home.'

I know his name, where he lives, his love of jogging, but that doesn't mean I know I can trust him.

He switches off the headlights, but leaves the engine running. The car door opens then clicks shut. I hear his footsteps coming towards me. I want to run, but my feet refuse to move. I stand still, waiting. He's almost reached me and my heart is hammering like a piston. I feel his hand reach for mine. It's like an electric shock and I whip my hand away.

'You can't walk all the way back to town.'

I turn. He is smiling, a kind smile, not like the leer of a lecher like Finn.

I wouldn't normally get into a car with a stranger, but he's not really a stranger. I make the decision. 'OK.'

We walk back to his car, the one I've seen many times in Martha's driveway. Before we reach it, I turn on my mobile, just in case.

'I didn't have any luck with your earring,' he says when we're driving along. 'Did you?'

'Yes, thanks,' I say. 'It's safe.'

I almost tell him about the raven, but hold back and we drive on in silence.

Several times, I feel him glancing at me in the darkness and I sneak a peek at him from time to time, too. He's quite good-looking and I try and stop myself feeling attracted to him. After the Finn fiasco, I don't need to make another miserable mistake, but I can't help feeling drawn to him. Am I still bewitched? Is it possible that he's attracted to me?

I need not have worried about my safety. He's as good as his word. I give him directions and he stops outside my lodging house. I climb out.

'Thanks again,' I say as I close the car door. I'm relieved he doesn't suggest coming in or seeing me again. That would have spoiled it.

It's almost one in the morning. I take off my shoes and tiptoe upstairs. I don't want Velcro waking up and questioning me. Once inside my room, I peel off the dress and the rest of the jewellery, let down my hair and throw myself into bed, certain I won't get a wink of sleep.

34

It's ten o'clock when I wake. I yawn and snuggle lower under my covers. The first thing on my mind is Finn, and I shudder at the memory. It's quite depressing to realise how naïve I've been. To think I believed I was in love with him, daring to dream he would fall for me. Well, he fell for me all right, but not in the way I childishly hoped.

I sit bolt upright. I'd forgotten all about Martha's earring. I must go round to see her. I trust the large black bird carrying it in its beak *was* Corvus and that it has been safely returned. I'm in real trouble if not.

Leaping out of bed, I make a hasty visit to the bathroom, get dressed, brush my hair and do a quick job on my make-up. I collect up the rest of Martha's jewellery and lay it safely inside its box. Placing the box in my backpack, I turn on my mobile.

I'm about to dash downstairs when it bleeps. I've got a text. I glance at the screen. It's from Dad.

Ella. Ring home asap

How can I ring home? *She's* likely to answer it … but if … my brain somersaults and lands with a crash. Hands shaking, I sit on my bed and tap out our home phone number, fingers crossed that my evil step-mother won't answer it.

'Hello?' It's Dad.

'Hi, Dad. What's up?'

'Ella, thank god you've got my message.' His voice sounds strained, almost hysterical. 'I need … I … Can I come and pick you up?'

I'm torn, and hesitate before answering, then rush into verbal diarrhoea about having to go to Martha's. 'It's really vital that I go, Dad. I'll explain later … I won't be long … ' I'm feeling guilty already. He sounds like he needs me really badly. But a little voice inside my head asks me where was he when I needed him.

'OK … how about twelve o'clock?' he asks.

I think of twelve o'clock, midnight. I broke my promise. I let someone down. I have to set that right before meeting Dad.

'Only … it's Sonia … '

My imagination kicks into action. She's dead. Dad has murdered her. She's hanging by her talons from a high tower. She's been devoured by lions, or hopefully something worse.

'What about her?'

'Look, it's no good on the phone. I'll tell you when I see you.'

'All right, Dad, I'll meet you at the bandstand at noon.' I'm itching to know, but I have to sort out Martha's jewellery first.

'OK. Bye, Ella.'

'Bye.'

Trembling all over, I head for the stairs. Velcro opens his bedroom door as I hurry by.

'Ella, how did it go … ?'

'Can't stop.' I leap down the stairs two at a time. 'I'll tell you later.'

I don't hear his reply as I'm halfway out of the front door before he can speak. I run all the way to Martha's and arrive panting on her doorstep. I bend double, gasping for breath, feeling slightly sick. After a few moments, I reach up and knock on the door. It opens almost immediately.

'Hello?' Jack is standing in the doorway, a puzzled expression in his eyes.

I step back, tongue-tied. I hadn't expected to see him standing there. Then I remember. It's Sunday morning.

Jack's expression tells me he doesn't recognise me from last night. I'm just a scruffy-looking girl, a fellow jogger.

'Jack, who is it?' Martha's voice comes from somewhere inside.

He turns. 'A girl I've seen out jogging a couple of times,' he calls.

'Ask her what her name is.'

Jack turns back to me and lifts his eyebrows. 'Well, you heard her ... '

'Ella,' I say, smiling up at him.

'Ella,' he calls then his expression changes. He stares. 'Ella?'

I nod, lifting my hands and swirling my hair on top of my head.

'Well, don't keep her waiting on the doorstep, Jack,' Martha calls. 'Invite her in.'

Jack steps back and I walk past him into the hall. Corvus is in place, but there is something about the hunching of his shoulders that reminds me of the taxi driver. He winks then nods slightly.

'I'm in the kitchen,' Martha calls.

'That way,' Jack says, but I'm halfway along the corridor by then. He follows me. I can feel his bewilderment through the back of my head.

'Tea?' Martha asks.

I go to the sink, fill the kettle and put it on the stove. While we wait for it to boil I sit on my usual chair opposite Martha and she smiles at me. I smile back. I wonder if she knows about the earring.

Jack stands in the doorway, arms folded. 'What's going on?' he asks.

Martha beckons to him. 'Sit down. I guess you two would like me to introduce you properly.'

'We've already met.' Jack and I speak together, then laugh. It helps me relax a little.

Martha raises her eyebrows and smiles, almost as if she

knows what we're going to say. Jack sits down. Bit by bit, we tell her about how we'd seen each other jogging and then about meeting at Finn's party, though we miss out the part about Finn's behaviour.

'In the end,' says Jack, 'I gave Ella a lift home. She missed her taxi.'

'Corvus told me.'

Jack doesn't react. He must know about the magic and the raven.

I swallow hard. 'And did Corvus tell you about the earring, too?'

'Of course he did.' She reaches in her pocket. 'Here it is.' She holds the earring up in front of her and we all watch the feathers shimmer.

I have to bite my lip. The relief has made me tearful again. I pull out the box and hand it to her.

'I'm sorry I almost lost the earring,' I mutter. 'The other one is there, and the necklace and hair clasp. Thank you for lending them to me.'

Jack is wide-eyed. 'So that jewellery you were wearing last night belonged to … ?'

'Yes, dear. They are mine.' Martha turns to me. 'And I expect they made you look beautiful, didn't they?'

'Yes,' says Jack. 'They did.'

I feel the heat surge up my face. So Jack thought that, did he? He must be extremely disillusioned by what I look like this morning.

Martha breaks into the silence. 'So how was the handsome young man you fell for? Did he live up to expectations?'

I avoid looking at Jack. 'No. He was horrible.'

'Oh, I'm sorry, dear.' Martha's face droops. 'I *so* wanted to help.' She looks as if she really cares.

The kettle boils and I make tea, pouring out our two usual cups.

'Tea, Jack?' I ask without catching his eye.

'Why not? And would somebody tell me how Ella knows her way about the place so well?'

We lean on our elbows over cups of tea while Martha explains to Jack about everything since the day she fell down outside Luigi's café.

'I did wonder if someone was coming in to help you,' says Jack when she has finished. 'Thanks, Ella.'

I nod. 'But I never got to clean the turret room.'

'My room,' says Jack. 'It's a fantastic place. Would you like to see it?'

'Please.'

I follow Jack past Corvus, who winks again, and up the first flight of stairs then along the corridor and up the narrow second flight that curves round to the left towards the top. The arched door opens onto a small circular room. I take in the narrow bed, the table covered in papers, an open laptop, clothes littered all over the floor.

'Sorry, I'm not the tidiest … '

I laugh at the understatement and go to the window. It's a great view right over town.

Suddenly, I notice the time. It's 11.45 and there are still loads of questions I need to ask. But they will have to wait.

'Thank you for showing me. I was curious, that's all, but I have to go,' I say.

Jack must think I make a habit of dashing off, but I can't help that. I rush downstairs and back to the kitchen.

'Martha, I've had a call from Dad,' I say. 'I've promised to meet him. Something's happened at home.'

'Ah, good … to your step-mother, perhaps?' It's only a murmur, but I've heard her.

I narrow my eyes when I look at her. Has she been using her magic on Sonia, too? She really is an extraordinary old lady!

'I hope so.' I grin and bend to give her a hug. 'Thanks for everything.'

'Nice to have had your acquaintance,' Corvus mutters as I let myself out.

Why did he say that? It almost sounded as if he wouldn't see me again.

'Yours, too.'

I close the door and run. I'll be just in time to meet Dad.

35

Dad's sitting in the bandstand in exactly the same place as last time. He's leaning forward, elbows on knees, and he looks dishevelled, like an old tramp. Glancing up, he sees me coming. He runs down the steps and across the grass towards me, flinging his arms round me and crushing me to his chest.

'Oh, Ella.' He's crying. I've only seen him cry a couple of times before, when Mum's cancer was diagnosed and after she died. I start crying too, my tears soaking his coat, though exactly why we're crying I'm not sure.

I wait for him to calm down. He lets me go and we both dry our tears. We begin to walk around the park. I don't speak, letting him tell me in his own time.

'What a mess!' The words rush out like a violent wind. 'How could I have been so stupid?'

I link my arm through his. He turns to look at me. There is a watery shine in his eyes and a wild look that I guess is not caused by the tears. Something traumatic has happened, something to do with Sonia. In spite of my thoughts earlier, I hope he hasn't murdered her. I couldn't bear him to end up in jail.

'What a night!' He shudders. 'She'd been her usual self, picking holes in everything I did, disagreeing with everything I said. She accused me of still being in love with your mum. Of course, I couldn't deny it. I don't think I'll ever stop loving her.'

'Really, Dad?' I bite my lip hard, though I'm melting inside.

'Really. Anyway, I was wondering how much more of Sonia's lashing tongue I could stand when things changed. It was about ten o'clock. All of a sudden, she went berserk, as if a demon had got inside her.'

'Berserk?'

'She threw herself at me, claws out, trying to rip me apart.'

A vision of the vulture flashes in front of my eyes.

'I won't go into detail, Ella. She was manic. She attacked me, fighting tooth and nail, like a wild animal. I defended myself for ages, but she was so strong. I thought she was going to kill me. Eventually, I managed to dash upstairs and lock myself in the bathroom.'

I squeeze his arm. Poor Dad! No wonder he looks such a wreck this morning.

'I could hear her crashing about until well after midnight, then it went quiet. A bit later, I heard the front door slam.

I waited a while then dared to creep out. It was like the aftermath of World War III. And she left a note.'

He delves in his coat pocket and pulls out a sheet of paper covered in an untidy scrawl.

I've had enough, you pathetic apology of a man. I'll be seeing my solicitor in the morning. Just you wait. I'll pick your bones till there's nothing of you left.
Goodbye

'Good riddance!' I say, as a shiver shoots up my spine. 'But why did she suddenly go for you like that?'

Dad shrugs. 'Her tempers have been getting worse the past few months, but she's never been that bad. It was like some sorcery had got into her.'

I stare at him.

'Ella, what is it?'

'Nothing,' I say. But I can't help thinking of Martha. She's helped me in so many ways. Why not this, too?

We sit on a park bench.

'What did you have to do this morning that was so important?' Dad asks.

I take a deep breath. 'Well, it's really hard to explain,' I begin. 'A few weeks ago, I helped an old lady and she's been so kind to me. She lent me something and I had to return it this morning.'

I can't begin to explain her magic. He'll say I've gone crazy, like Velcro did.

'You hinted at that on the phone,' he says. 'Tell me about her. It'll take my mind off what's happened at home.'

Choosing my words carefully, I tell Dad as much as I dare.

'I'd like to meet her ... and thank her.'

'No, Dad.' I want to keep the different parts of my life separate if I can. 'She's just an old lady ... '

'We'll see.'

'So what are you going to do now?' I ask.

'See my solicitor. Beat her at her own game. It's going to be very messy, Ella. We're going to have to be very strong to get through this.'

I snuggle up to him, liking the way he used 'we', as if we're a family again.

My phone bleeps. I've got a message. It's from Jodie.

Yr dad OK? Police there last night

I read it out to Dad. 'You didn't tell me that,' I say.

'I called them out. They took loads of photos ... for evidence.' An enormous sigh shudders through his body. 'Oh, Ella, I never thought it would turn out like this. I'm sorry.'

I give him a hug. Telling me has done him good. He's looking a bit more like my old dad already, but even though Sonia has gone, I'm not going to rush into going home. Not quite yet, anyway.

After Dad has driven away, I reply to Jodie's text. I tell her Sonia's left. Immediately, the phone rings.

'Yay!' she yells. 'Great news!'

'Yeah. I've got so much to tell you ... It's been a rollercoaster of a few weeks.' I gabble on about an old lady who performs magic, a raven that becomes a taxi driver, a boy with body odour and revolting habits that I thought I fancied then found I didn't, and the mysterious Mr J, Jack, who I've only just met though I've been aware of him for ages.

When I pause for breath there is silence.

'Jodie, are you still there?'

'Yes ... just! I'm reeling ... are you living in a circus? Or a nuthouse?'

I laugh. 'I knew you wouldn't understand a word I was talking about. How about meeting up for coffee tomorrow?'

'School,' she says. 'Have you forgotten? I still attend that dump, even if you don't! I'm the keen A-level student – not!! But I reckon I could bunk off at break time. Can you get over to Barnfield? Ten-thirty in the café on the corner?'

'OK.'

I'm smiling as I ring off and I almost skip along the road, back to the house.

Velcro is there, waiting for me. He's frowning as he hands me an envelope. It's addressed to Miss Ella Sharma in large scrawling writing.

'Delivered by hand,' he says. 'I think it was the same bloke as drove that taxi last night.'

Corvus? I feel a cold shiver as I rip it open and begin to read.

36

My dear, lovely Ella
My work is done. Corvus and I have to move on. That is
the nature of my existence, although I sometimes wonder if I am
getting rather old and infirm for this. I hope you have enjoyed our
friendship as much as we have enjoyed yours. I have grown
extremely fond of you, but I cannot let that stand in my way.

I collapse into a chair. I can't believe what I've just read.
Is Martha saying goodbye? I'm aware of Velcro watching me, a
frown on his freckled face. Hands shaking, I focus on the words
in front of me.

When I embarked upon our relationship, it began with a forlorn, lonely girl who had lost her way. It's finishing with a beautiful, honest, much happier and more confident girl with a lot to look forward to.

I'm not sure about the beautiful bit, but the rest is true. I *am* a different person to when I met her.

I know there are many unanswered questions in your mind, so I will try to answer some of them.

I nod. Martha's dead right. I'd love to know more.

Corvus has been my assistant for over sixty years. He comes alive at appropriate moments, but, like the pumpkin, his magic can only last for a limited amount of time.

I smile, remembering his odd behaviour sitting at the bottom of Martha's stairs, and I'll never forget him as the taxi driver on the night of the party.

I hate to see unhappiness. So when I saw your dejected face at the window of that café on that dark, wet November afternoon and realised that you were making a wish as you stirred your coffee, I recognised it as a call for help.

I swallow hard, trying to keep my emotions in check. Velcro opens his mouth to speak, but I shake my head. I know he means well, but I don't want to be interrupted, however painful the letter is.

And so, dear Ella, I must say goodbye. When we met, you had no one to turn to, except that nice young man who lives in your lodging house. You were suffering from the evil of your step-mother, a temporary loss of your father's affections, and also mourning your mother, which you will continue to do for a very long time, I know. However, you have your father's love again, now we have rid him of that monstrous predatory woman. You and your father can mourn together by sharing those wonderful memories you obviously have of the person you both loved so much.

A warm feeling spreads through me. There are so many things I need to thank her for and she is right. I've got my Dad back!

As for your unfortunate experience with that conceited Adonis, Finn, I'm sorry to say that my magic must have gone slightly askew in making you fall for him. I actually had other ideas.

I can't help smiling at that. So Martha admits it was her fault that I fell for Finn.

I am sure you must have been wondering about Jack. He is my beloved grandson …

I might have guessed!

... whose parents live on the other side of the world. Jack has lived with me for many years.

I am convinced that he is already showing some kind of affection for you. He will not be leaving Madebury, but is moving into an apartment which I have found for him in the town. He knows where you live and you will meet again.

I feel suddenly hot. Has Martha lined me up with him now?

Don't be sad. Think of me as your Fairy Godmother who came when you most needed me. Now that you need me no longer, I must go.

I will always remember you with much affection.
Your loving friend
Martha

37

Dropping the letter on the table, I slump into a chair and bury my head in my hands. Velcro takes the letter and hurriedly reads it.

'So you weren't making it all up,' he mutters. 'Incredible!'

'She can't do this!' I leap up, grip the letter in my hand and dash to the door. 'Perhaps she hasn't gone yet.'

Velcro follows me from the house, panting and grumbling at my speed as I head towards Martha's road.

Outside her gate, I stumble to a stop and stare through the metalwork. Curtains have been closed and there is no sign of life. I run towards the house, climb the porch steps and bang on the door.

'Martha!' I call through the letter box. 'Corvus! Are you there?'

My voice echoes back at me from a hollow, empty place.

Velcro is waiting at the gate.

'Come home, Ella,' he calls. 'There's no one there, can't you see?'

I refuse to believe him. Pushing my way through the overgrown garden, I rush around the house, trying doors and stretching up to look in windows, but the doors are locked and all the windows are the same, curtains closed. Sadly, I return to the front and sit on the steps, hoping that if I wait long enough, Martha will open the door. Through misty eyes, I watch Velcro pacing up and down on the pavement, hunched shoulders, hands in pockets, kicking at the gold and brown leaves.

'Are you coming?' he calls.

'No!' I can't believe Martha has gone, so suddenly and without warning.

The black cat slinks over to me and rubs the side of his face on my legs.

'So you haven't gone,' I say, stroking his back and feeling the purr through my fingers. 'Why hasn't Martha taken you with her?'

The cat blinks and slowly disappears into the jungle of garden.

Velcro has grown tired of waiting. 'See you later then,' he calls as he walks away.

I'm still gripping Martha's letter. Smoothing it out, I read it over again, several times.

A car horn makes me jump and I look up. A car has stopped outside the gate. Someone is getting out. Jack!

I leap down the steps and throw myself at him. He hugs me. Then I step back, embarrassed.

'Sorry,' I mutter, 'but I'm so pleased to see you. Where has Martha gone?'

He shrugs. 'Wherever she's needed,' he says. 'She's been like this ever since I can remember.'

'But ... '

'Mind you, she's really fond of you ... she said you're very special.'

'I've grown fond of her, too.'

'She also said ... ' He stops mid-sentence and looks down at his feet.

'What?'

'Oh, nothing.' There's a hint of a smile as his eyes meet mine, but also something else in his expression that makes my heart flutter.

Then Jack turns away. He opens the boot of his car and pulls out a cat basket.

'Help me catch Gus, will you?'

'He's your cat, then? I wondered why Martha hadn't taken him with her.'

As we hunt for Gus in the garden, a blackbird begins to sing in the tree above us, a beautiful musical sound. I stop to listen.

'I love birdsong,' I say, 'especially the blackbird. My mum loved it, too.'

Jack doesn't reply and I'm glad. He seems to understand

what I'm feeling right now. Maybe, one day, I'll be able to tell him everything.

We laugh a lot as we dive through bushes, get snagged on brambles and stung by nettles, but eventually we catch Gus. Jack manages to push him, complaining, into the basket, which he puts back in the boot.

He grins. 'Come on, Ella,' he says. 'I'll take you home.'

I grin back, aware that I'm blushing again, and climb into his car.

Epilogue

Dear Cecily

How are you, dear? I've almost settled in my new home, but I'm afraid I'm still quite unsteady on my pins. I really must remember to take my stick with me next time I go out. I fell over again, you see, right there in the High Street. If it weren't for a girl picking me up, I don't know how I would have got home.

Cindy, she said her name was. A strange girl, gaunt, sad. I think she must be going through some kind of crisis. I can't make out what the problem is, but she fascinates me ...